Bendigo Gold

More things that kids said:

Brilliant! You want to hear more

I like the stories inside the story

It kept you guessing

It's like you are in the story

It's in the top three books that I've read

It's better than other books

Published by Shedels Ireland 2015
www.shedels.weebly.com

Printed by Lettertec
www.lettertecbooks.ie

All rights reserved. No part of this publication may be reproduced, stored in a retrieval system, or transmitted by any means, electronic, mechanical, photocopying, recording or otherwise, without the prior permission of the copyright holder.

ISBN 978-0-9930914-1-4

Text Copyright: Heather Smith 2015

Cover Design: Will Dahm

This book is a work of fiction. Names, characters, places and incidents are either the product of the author's imagination or are used factiously, and any resemblance to actual persons, living or dead, business establishments, events or locales is entirely coincidental.

Bendigo Gold

HEATHER SMITH

SHEDELS BOOKS

Thank you

A huge thank you to all the people who helped me to write and produce Bendigo Gold. Thank you to Justine Finn for her legal advice and critical appraisal; to Sarah Webb, Irish author, Sandra Glover, Cornerstones, and Marianne Gunn O'Connor, Creative Agency, for their expertise and directives; to the people in Bendigo who helped with accuracy issues, especially Carol Holsworth, Craig Kendal and Sandra Thomson; to Will Dahm for his offbeat cover to match this offbeat book; to Heather Fleming for assistance with typing challenges; to Kirsty Tobin for proofreading; to Andrew Haworth, Lettertec Printing; to Dorothy Verplanke, Sara Good, Meriel and Craig Rankin, and other members of my family and friends for their encouragement; and especially to my husband, Robin, for tolerating my moods when I was writing.

But, above all...

Thank you to all the children who piloted my book

Thank you for the suggestions that changed the focus of this book, and thank you for the generosity of your comments that surprised me and warmed my soul.

CHAPTER 1
THE ENVELOPE

I wiggled it just a tiny bit more and out it came – a large envelope, wrinkled, cobwebbed and yellowed with age.

"What are you up to now?" asked Granny.

"Just collecting yesteryear's post for you," I replied, straightening up. "It was stuck behind the cupboard."

I placed the envelope on the table.

To my darling May
From Pa O'Neill
January 2000

"Oh Granny," I said. "A letter from a secret admirer."

She lifted the envelope, shifted her glasses to the correct position on her nose and peered at the label. "Pa O'Neill, well I never..." she murmured, as memories seemed to flit through her brain. "What a surprise!"

She sat back, idly examining the cover.

"Was he special?" I teased.

"Very special," she replied. Turning to me with a smile, she said, "Pa was an old boy at the nursing home... In his eighties when I first met him. Special, but hardly a romantic liaison."

She rubbed a cobweb off the envelope.

"I wonder why he sent you the letter," I said, peeking over her shoulder.

"Well, the same wondering thought was crossing my mind too," she replied, beginning to stand up. "But..."

I was in like a shot.

"Will I open it for you?" I asked.

"I suppose you can," replied Granny with a twinkle as she sat down again and carefully placed the envelope on the table, "but let's have a cup of tea first."

I got out two cups, popped two Barry's tea bags into them, squeezed out the bags, added a drop of milk to each and handed her one.

"He was an old miner from Australia," she said, settling into the chair. "We used to have great old chats."

"But how come he left the envelope behind the cupboard?" I asked.

Taking no notice of my question, she said, "He was delighted when he heard I had been an O'Neill before I married." She gazed absentmindedly out the window, then continued. "He was fascinated by the connection."

"And I bet he enjoyed all your stories," I said, picking up the envelope.

"Oh yes," she replied. "Names and stories link people together, but he was a born storyteller himself, too."

I put the envelope to my nose and smelled the musty paper.

"A rock broke his leg during a blast and it never mended properly. He was one of those people who never complained. He just hobbled around with a stick." Granny looked at the envelope in my hand. "He was a lovely person."

"It's strange how the envelope got behind the cupboard," I said, hoping that her cup of tea was nearly finished.

"Oh, he used to come out here visiting occasionally. He'd come for afternoon tea and I'd drop him back afterwards."

"But how did the envelope get behind the cupboard?" I asked, trying to fast forward to the opening.

"I've absolutely no idea," said Gran, "except that he had a bit of a turn the last day he was here, and hit his head off the cupboard when he was falling."

"Well, that's probably when it happened." I said, placing the envelope directly in front of Granny.

"Perhaps," she replied. "He died shortly after."

I nudged the envelope forward. "Have you finished your tea yet, Granny?"

"Just about," she said, taking another sip. "You know, Emily," she said, leaning towards me, "I think he was the first person who ever really listened to me. Most people are just too busy."

I wished she'd hurry up, but I knew it was absolutely no use rushing Granny.

"I used to chat to him for ages about the family," she continued.

"And all about me," I added.

"Of course. You were born a month before he died."

"And about Daddy and Mummy's accident?"

"I told him everything," she replied, looking directly at me. "He was that kind of man."

Granny hesitated. "Most people never really listen."

I guiltily put another tea bag in her cup. "Another cuppa?"

"He was a good man," she said, forgetting to reply. Then, tapping the table for attention, she asked, "Did you know, Emily, I was born somewhere near Melbourne?"

"Sure," I said, wondering where the heck it was.

"But I'm more Irish than Australian, because my mother brought me back to Ireland when I was six."

I could feel Granny slipping back into story mode.

"Yes, I know," I said quickly before she had time to start on a new story. "It was because your mum was sick and the aunts sent her the fare home."

She sighed and I guessed I was going to hear all about her father, the old jailbird, again, so I pushed the envelope towards her.

"The post," I said. "Years late!"

Stolen from her thoughts, Granny laughed, slipped her finger through the tiny hole at the top of the cover and ripped open the envelope.

CHAPTER 2
A FLASH FROM THE PAST

As Gran ran her finger along the yellowed gum of the seal, she shook the contents out on the table.

"What have we here?" she asked, pulling two smaller envelopes out of the large envelope. "Hmm," she said. "That one looks official and this one is marked 'Private'. Which one will we open first?"

"You open one and I'll open the other," I suggested.

"Would you like to open the official one or the private one?" She arched her eyebrow.

"Since the private one is from your special boyfriend, I suppose I'd better read the official one," I said with a grin.

"Then I'm sure you'll wish me to read my private letter first," she countered.

"Of course," I said, wishing Granny wasn't such a tease as she gave me a wink, flicked open her letter with a flourish and began to read.

As I watched, Granny's face began to crumble. She turned an ashen white and her hands began to shake. She looked at me – or, should I say, past me – and covered her mouth. "Oh dear, oh dear... Why didn't he tell me?" she whispered.

"Tell you what?" I asked, hearing the shock in her voice.

She lifted the letter and continued to read to herself. "He never told me."

I rubbed her elbow. "Told you what, Granny?"

She took off her glasses and covered her entire face with her hands.

"What's wrong, Granny?" I asked, as my heart began to thump. I'd never seen her so agitated and upset.

"If only I'd known," she said, as she silently began to rock to and fro.

Then she seemed to cry. She didn't make a big lot of noise like I do when I cry. All her sobs seemed locked inside and they didn't seem to be able to escape. I didn't know what to do.

I'm twelve and I know twelve year olds are meant to be able to handle situations, but when a Granny cries, things are seriously wrong, and I hadn't a clue what to do. I tried to comfort her, but she didn't seem to even notice I was there.

I waited for a few moments and then I said as calmly as I could, "Granny, if you tell me what the problem is, perhaps I'll be able to help you."

She looked at me strangely, her lip quivering. "It's Pa," she said. "He was my friend. The old boy who used to listen to me... but he wasn't just my friend. He was..." She paused, trying to catch her breath. "He was my Pa... My real Pa... my father."

I stared at her.

Imagine that. Pa O'Neill being Granny's real Pa... and she not knowing it all those years. Even I found that difficult to take in.

"Are you sure?" I asked.

"Why didn't he just tell me?" said Granny quietly to herself. "If only I'd known."

"Well, you didn't," I replied stoutly, feeling more like a mother than a child. "What does he say in the letter?"

"Here it is. You read it," she said, pushing the letter in my direction. "Just read it yourself."

I took the letter and began to read:

Dear May,

Please forgive a silly old man for not telling you a secret. I couldn't share it with you because I was afraid it would destroy our friendship. You see, I gradually discovered from all the stories you told me about the family that I am your father – your real father. I am the jailbird and the drunk your aunts told you about.

I glanced at Gran. "You didn't know," I said.

"Ah," she said, her voice trembling. "I didn't spare the poor man. The aunts always told me that my father was a drunken lout... and that's how I've always thought of him."

"Granny," I said, "it wasn't your fault. He never told you."

"He was such a nice old gent," she whispered. "Why didn't he just tell me? I'd have brought him out of the home. He could have lived with me."

I put my arms around Gran. "I'm sure he knew you were fond of him."

"Perhaps," Gran replied, her voice filling with sadness. "But I told him I hated my father. Hated him because he never came back to get me."

"But you didn't know, Granny," I said.

She shook her head and disappeared into her own thoughts, her eyes filling with tears. There was nothing I could do. I'm just a child and there was nothing I could do to help my Granny, so I took that terrible letter and wandered into the next room. It was time for me to discover my past. Time to learn about my missing great-grandfather, Pa O'Neill.

CHAPTER 3
THE PRIVATE LETTER

I sat by the window, opened the strange letter and continued to read:

I met your mam, Millicent, at a dance back in 1944. She was the most beautiful girl I had ever seen and we were married within the year. Times were tough after the war and, in 1945, we moved to Bendigo, just north west of Melbourne in Australia. We bought the homestead from Phil Hannigan, an old prospector in Back Creek. I got a job as a miner down Central Deborah Mine and your mam worked part time in Woolworths, and, at the weekends, we'd go out travelling on the tram, or we might go dancing down at The Shamrock with our friend Matt Henson.

You were born in 1946. You had lots of beautiful curls and big blue eyes and I loved you and your mam with all my heart.

Winter came, and a great storm knocked down the old gum by the creek. When I went down to check the damage, there, hidden in the roots of the tree, was a nugget of gold. Your mam and I were wild with excitement, but, after jumping around for a bit, we hid the gold in case the hordes of gold diggers would descend on us. We said we'd keep it for when we'd need it.

You used to love the colour of the nugget, so I often took it out to show it to you, but, one day, the nugget went missing. Your mam and I searched everywhere, but we could not find it. We were sure it had been stolen from us, but what could we do about it?

The door opened and there was Granny standing like a statue, her eyes fixed on the letter as I started to read aloud.

Shortly after, I myself was accused of stealing gold from the mine. That was a serious offence. I was framed and there was nothing I could do. I lost my job as a miner and I was thrown into jail for two years.

I stopped reading. "He was framed, Granny."

"So he says," she replied, "but the aunts had a different story."

I read the last paragraph again. "Somebody definitely framed him," I repeated, continuing to read.

They were the longest two years of my life. Your mam got sick and she went home to Ireland with you. Then I heard that both of you had died on the voyage. It was terrible, and when I came out of jail, I was good for nothing except drinking.

There was silence.

"Granny," I said, "he thought you were dead." I peeked at Granny out of the corner of my eye. She was gripping the back of the chair, and she seemed smaller.

"So that's why he didn't come back," she was whispering to herself. "He thought I had died."

"Yes," I said, returning to the letter.

I wouldn't have lasted if a friend hadn't dragged me to church. My whole life changed and I became a new man. I went back to our little homestead in Back Creek and tidied it up. I weeded the garden and rebuilt the old walls that had fallen down. Your mam would have been proud of me.

I stopped for a breath.

"Go on, child," she said, beckoning me to continue.

One day, I was down by the bridge replacing a few stones that had come away in the last flood. The bridge was beside your playhouse. Do you remember? Well, I was just pushing in a loose stone when I spotted it. There it was, as nice as you like, behind one of the stones in the bridge. I couldn't believe it. My nugget of gold. The lump of gold you were so fond of... I held it in my hand.

"Would you read that bit about finding the nugget?" Gran asked, her voice shaking slightly. "Read it again, out loud."

"No bother," I replied, wondering what was going on in her head. When I'd read the piece, she asked me to read it one more time.

"Sure," I obliged. "And then will I read to the end of the letter?"

"Yes," she said. "Please do."

The years passed by, the recession bit and, one day, I just decided to go home to Ireland. I didn't even bother selling the place. Nobody wanted it. So, I simply packed my bags and left.

When I got home, I visited the old aunts' place, and one of the neighbours told me that you lived with them before they died. I couldn't believe it... All those years wasted thinking that you were dead. I tried to find you, but you had moved on and married, and nobody seemed to know your married name.

Granny was listening intently to everything I read, but this time I could feel something happy growing inside her.

I stayed in the locality and finally ended up in St Carmel's Home. I thought I'd never see you again but, one day, you came in with the library books. You'd been living close by the whole time. I wanted to tell you who I was, but I couldn't. The aunts had poisoned you against me, and I didn't think you'd believe my story. So I just listened to you. How I loved your stories and how I loved your kindness.

You, my dear, are very like your darling mother.
Take care.
Your loving father,
Pa

PS I guess you found a good hiding spot for that lump of gold!

I looked at Granny. There was a touch of a smile around her lips.

"Good gracious, I did it," she said, slowly. "All those years ago, I hid the nugget of gold. I remember now. I hid it in the wall so I could play with it whenever I wanted to."

"Oh no," I said in a shocked voice. "And you never told them?"

"No, I was too frightened," she replied, covering her mouth. "They were so cross about someone stealing it."

I just stared at her. "Oh Granny," I muttered. "I'm surprised at you."

"I just didn't understand," she said. "I suppose I was only five or six at the time and I just didn't understand. And then Dad went into jail."

I looked at my gran, who was biting her lip. "So you never told your mother?"

"I was young, and I suppose I just forgot about the lump of gold."

I could see a glimmer of a smile beginning to appear again. "Until now," she said, walking to the window. "Isn't it strange how buried memories can suddenly pop up again? It's all a bit of a shock."

I looked at my gran, and it suddenly struck me that I was very like her. "You can say that again," I said.

She turned around. "And to think that old rascal knew I had hidden the nugget all that time ago!"

"I don't suppose," I said, suddenly thinking about the important things in life, "that you know where the nugget of gold is now?"

"Gracious, no," said Granny, wrinkling her forehead. "I've absolutely no idea what happened to it."

I picked up the second letter and presented it to her.

"Do you think this would be a good time to read the official letter?"

"Perhaps," she said, cautiously handing it back to me.

CHAPTER 4
THE OFFICIAL LETTER

And, no. There wasn't a big fat nugget of gold in the official letter. I wish you were right, but you weren't.

There wasn't even a treasure map showing the whereabouts of the gold.

No, inside the letter was a very official looking will. A truly unbelievable will. A will that would change our lives.

Gran took the document and began to read:

This is the last will and testament of Patrick O'Neill of Hermitage Rest, Garryduff, in the City of Cork, Ireland. I hereby revoke all previous wills and testamentary dispositions made by me. I appoint as my solicitor Jim Good of Patrick's Hill, Cork, as executor of this will and direct him to pay my just debts, funeral and testamentary expenses.

To my daughter, May Clancy of Rock View, Garryduff, Cork, Ireland I bequeath my property, 'Rainbow End', in

Back Creek, Bendigo, Victoria, Australia. The nugget of gold found at Back Creek, Bendigo, Victoria, Australia, and all the residue and remainder of my property of any nature and description, and wherever situated, I bequeath to my great-granddaughter, Emily McCleary of Rock View, Garryduff, Cork, Ireland.

Dated this 4th day of May 2000
Signed Pa O'Neill

Signed by the testator as and for his last will and testament in the presence of us, both present at the same time, and signed by us in the presence of the testator.

Ken Hosford
Lane Giles

There was silence for a moment and then I leaped into the air.

"Granny," I screamed, dancing around the place. "We're rich!"

"My goodness," Gran said. "I don't believe it."

She placed the will on the table with a shaky hand and moved over to the window. She stood there, gazing in amazement out into the garden.

"Granny, we're rich!" I screamed again, as I jigged around the kitchen. "We'll never again have to pretend. We'll be able to pay for everything."

Granny looked strangely at me. There was a stunned look in her eye. Finally, she went back over to the table, picked up the will again and read it to herself for the second time.

"That's incredible," she said, running her fingers through her hair. "Whoever would have thought it?" Then she went over to her chair and sat down. I wondered what was going to happen next.

"Don't you understand, Granny?" I said, grabbing her hand and shaking it. "Pa has given you Rainbow End and he's given me the nugget of gold. We're going to be rich. You're going to be able to pay all the bills."

I badly wanted Granny to start smiling again, but she seemed far away in a world of her own.

"You don't need to worry anymore. You'll be able to pay the book bill and the electricity bill and the heating bill and the phone bill and the grocery bill and... and everything else as well.

Still, Granny didn't move. She seemed pinned to the chair. She had just got over the shock of discovering who Pa really was, and now she was in shock from the will.

"We're going to be okay." I said rubbing her arm. "Granny, can you hear me? Everything is going to work out."

There was a stillness about Granny, but I knew something was beginning to register in her mind when I saw her lips quiver. Otherwise, she didn't move a muscle as she sat in her chair.

I forced myself to calm down as I sat down on the floor. My head felt as if it would burst, but I shut my mouth firmly and waited.

Children are good at waiting, aren't they? I waited and I waited.

Nothing happened.

I stood up and fed the dog. Nothing happened.

I washed the dishes and laid the table for tea. Still, nothing happened.

I sat down on the floor at her feet and looked up at her.

Then, eventually, something happened. She looked down at me, tilted her head to one side and lifted one eyebrow, and I spotted a twinkle appear in her eye.

"I wonder where the nugget of gold is now. I wonder if it's still in my secret hiding place," she said.

The thought had crossed my mind too, as I waited, but I said nothing.

"Oh dear," she said. "You have a terrible Granny"

And next minute, she started to giggle. It started out as a tiny little giggle and it began to grow. It started to bubble. I'd never seen a Granny change so much in such a short space of time. My Granny was now laughing quietly and the laughter was growing into something a bit hysterical... the sort of behaviour you don't expect from a Granny.

She stretched back in the chair and it began to rock as the bubbling turned into fits of laughter. She couldn't stop. She just shook in the chair, crying with helpless laughter. The room became full of merriment and I couldn't help joining in.

She grabbed me in a big hug, danced me around the kitchen, plopped me on the chair and said, "What a strange and wonderful man. I just can't believe it." Then she gave me a big kiss.

"It's incredible," she said. "Such a coincidence. All that time I was chatting to him, I never dreamed I was speaking to my dad."

She stared at her two letters in amazement. "What class of a person pretends he isn't your dad and then leaves you a farm of land in a foreign country, and a nugget of gold for your granddaughter?"

"Maybe," I said cautiously, "Rainbow End was sold years ago, and maybe there's no nugget of gold anymore."

"Maybe," said Granny coming down to earth, "but I was born in Rainbow End and I remember holding the nugget in my hand. Of course, who owns them now is another question altogether, but I think, Miss Emily McCleary, it's time to visit that solicitor Mr Jim Good and find out.

"And let's..." she said, tilting her chin. "Let's get a bank loan and go to Australia. Let's find Rainbow End and that nugget of gold. It's time to have an adventure. What do you say, Emily?"

"That would be okay with me," I said.

CHAPTER 5
MY FLYING COMPANION

And that was that. Four weeks later we were sitting in the plane on our way to Melbourne. Qantas Airlines calls it the Kangaroo Route.

Granny had organised the passports, the visas and the tickets, and we were on our way to check out Rainbow End in a strange place called Bendigo.

I lounged back in my seat. It was the first time I'd flown, and this was going to be the adventure of a lifetime.

Then I saw him, sauntering down the aisle with this intense expression, and I knew, without any shadow of a doubt, that the guy was going to sit beside me. Right enough, he peered at all the numbers of the seats and eventually ended up beside our row.

"This is the one," he announced, and he plopped himself down beside me, took out a stick of chewing gum and began to chew. His mother sat down beside him, smiled at me and busied herself tying her safety belt.

"I'm glad you've got each other for company," she murmured. "It's such a long journey."

Just my luck, I thought taking out my book to read.

My new companion produced his Nintendo DS and began to play a game, one robot annihilating the other robot as he twiddled away with the controls.

Soon, the flight was under way and, after the Qantas staff had done the safety drill with us, they came around and offered us drinks. They were very friendly, but, when they bent over and offered the boy beside me a drink, he just said, "Coke," in a very dismissive voice. No mention of please or thank you.

Later, when they brought meals along on their trolleys, he just said, "Chicken". When he got the meal, he picked through the food, spat out some and rejected the rest.

I glanced across at him. 'What a pleasant chap and what wonderful manners,' I thought… and that was before he rolled up his chewing gum and glued it under his table.

I deliberately distracted myself so I wouldn't be watching him. Then, suddenly, without any invitation, he said, "Ask me anything you like about gold."

"Gold?"

"I know everything about Australian gold."

"Fabulous! But what makes you think I'd want to ask you anything about it?" I couldn't credit his ill manners.

"You're going to Bendigo, so you'll need to know," he replied in a matter of fact voice.

"Just because you were listening to my conversation with my granny, doesn't mean I want you to teach me about gold."

"It does," he replied. "You're very ignorant."

I bit my tongue before replying. "You may be right, but what business is it of yours?"

"None," he responded, "but I fancy your sweets."

"What?"

"I saw Werther's in your bag and I'd like them."

"So you think I'll give them to you? You must be joking."

"Ask me any question you like about gold, and if I am 100 percent right, you'll have to give me the sweets."

"And if you're not 100 percent right, you'll have to lend me your Nintendo DS for an hour."

"No problem."

"Alright, Mr Know-It-All. What if I give you a rapid-fire quiz?"

"No problem."

I smiled inwardly. I had actually been to the library recently. I had visited the 'Mining' section, specifically, and I had jotted down a lot of information about gold exploration in Australia. Even if I wasn't brilliant at remembering all the facts, I had all the information in this little notebook in my bag. I rooted around at the bottom of my bag, found the book and opened it.

"You ready?"

"Ready and waiting," he replied. So I let him have it.

CHAPTER 6
RAPID FIRE

My flying companion arranged himself in his seat.

"I haven't got all day, you know," he said.

"That makes two of us. Can't wait to have a go on your Nintendo," I replied.

He bent his head and screwed his eyes in concentration as I started shooting those questions at him as fast as I could fire them. Let me tell you, these questions were challenging. And if you don't believe me, just try them on your friends.

"Still ready?" I inquired, fastening my eyes on the back of his head.

He nodded.

"Okay," I said, "I'll begin with a couple of easy ones. Which gold town is known as 'Big Gold Mountain', and what is alluvial gold?"

"Bendigo, and gold found along the riverbanks."

"Getting a bit harder. What do 'The Hand of Faith' and 'The Welcome Stranger' have in common, and why was the goldfield Ophir famous?"

"They are both nuggets of gold and Ophir was the first official goldfield in Australia. Have you any difficult questions?"

"Name four places where gold was found in Australia."

Without drawing breath, he replied, "Bendigo, Ballarat, Kalgoorlie and Coolgardie."

"Who was the first person to find gold near Bendigo?"

"Margaret Kennedy in 1851." He yawned.

"Where would you find 'The Super Pit'?"

"Kalgoorlie," the maggot replied, staring at my Werther's sweets and not even pretending to concentrate anymore.

"Number 8," I said, curling my lip. "Explain the following: prospector, golden mile, shafts, poppet heads, drives, sluice boxes, panning, claims and miners' licences."

"Gold digger, goldmine in Kalgoorlie, holes, cranes, tunnels, washing cradles, separating ore, prospectors' land and permission to prospect."

I looked at him in utter amazement. I couldn't believe it. He'd got them all right. I rooted around in my notebook for a few even harder questions. The next ones were stinkers.

I smiled. "Are you ready to roll again?"

"To roll?" he asked, puzzled. "Roll where?"

"Nowhere," I replied. "It's just a figure of speech."

"Oh," he said. "Why don't you say what you mean?"

'Fool,' I thought. "Are you ready to continue?" I asked in my best English.

"Ready and waiting," he replied.

"Name the Irish gold prospectors who found gold near Kalgoorlie."

"Paddy Hannon, Dan Shea and Tom Flanagan."

"What is open pit mining?"

My companion sneered. "Mining done in the open air. Isn't that fairly self-explanatory?"

"Just answer the questions," I snapped. "What type of mine is the Central Deborah Mine?"

"A quartz reef gold mine."

"During the gold rush, how much did a licence cost?"

"Thirty shillings a month."

"During the gold rush what size was a claim?"

"3.6 metres square."

"Where is Sovereign Hill?" I asked, fishing around in my bag for more questions.

"Ballaret."

"Why were the Chinese miners disliked?"

"They were hard workers, ate different food, wore strange clothes and had a foreign culture and customs."

I blinked. Those Werther's were history unless I upped my game. My rapid-fire quiz simply wasn't working. What was I to do? I tried a few more shockers.

"What effect did the Australian gold rush have on Australia?"

"Immigration, multi-culturalism and racism increased."

I couldn't believe his answer. I mean, does anybody out there have a clue what words like immigration, multi-culturalism and racism mean? I looked up. He was waiting expectantly, staring at me.

I began to stutter.

"Which state currently produces the most gold per year?"

"Western Australia produces over 70 percent of the gold."

Those last two questions were absolute rotters and guess what? He'd got them absolutely right. Can you imagine that? 100 percent correct. He was a genius... A freaky genius. I looked across in desperation at Granny. She smiled sweetly back at me. I'd run out of questions, but I could see she wasn't going to help me.

"You're on your own," she said. "It's between the two of you."

What was I to do? I bit my lip as I rummaged again in my bag in a vain search for the killer question. Then I spotted a price tag stuck on to a pair of socks.

'Ah ha,' I thought. 'I have it.'

"Last question," I announced, grinning. "What, may I ask, was the price of gold in, let's say... the summer of 2011?"

He looked at me, quizzically.

'Goody,' I thought. 'I have him.'

"That's an unreasonable question," he said.

"Why so?" I asked.

"Because it varied. Give me an exact date."

So I did just that and, off the top of my head, I said, "The 8th of August, 2011."

And, you know what? He thought for a few seconds and then said, "There was a dramatic drop in share prices at that time. People stopped investing in risky ventures because the currencies in different countries were crumbling and they decided to put their money into gold, so the price for gold on that day shot up to $1,700 per ounce."

I just looked at him. I couldn't dispute it, because I simply didn't know. He was unbelievable. Granny started to laugh. How did his head hold so much information? It made me sick.

"The Werther's," he said, with his hand out and a smug look.

I can tell you for nothing that I didn't congratulate him. I simply produced the Werther's, gave them to him in silence, then got out my book and continued to read with my back turned to him. And you know what? The maggot didn't even notice. He got out his Nintendo DS again, and the robots continued murdering each other as he ate my sweets. All of my sweets. The delicious sweets that I'd been saving. Every single last one of them, by himself.

CHAPTER 7
A BRUSH WITH THE BUSH

Finally, after flying for nearly 23 hours, travelling approximately 17,000 kilometres, passing through at least nine time zones, crossing more than ten countries, stopping for about two hours in Hong Kong, watching four movies, finishing two books and lots of magazines, eating four meals, drinking six bottles of orange, and trotting to the toilet four times, eventually we reached our destination – Melbourne.

The airport was buzzing with people. Instead of leading a dog, everybody seemed to be leading a suitcase – big ones, little ones, gaudy ones, drab ones, bulgy ones, slim-line ones... Every type of case.

Some of their owners wore shorts and t-shirts, and others wore jeans, jackets and scarves. Some tottered along on high heels, wearing short tube dresses and loads of lipstick, while others looked plain shabby. But everybody had attitude and I loved it!

Granny's baggage got lost and that caused a bit of a flurry, until we discovered that the maggot had mistaken it for his baggage. The bag was duly returned. No apologies were offered. The maggot's mother showed no surprise that her brilliant son had picked up the wrong bag, and the brilliant boy showed no remorse for the inconvenience he had caused. He didn't even notice my smug, self-satisfied expression, but Granny gave me a wink and that was enough.

I picked up the bag and we headed over to the car rental office. Granny sorted out the paperwork and we picked up brochures from the information desk, collected the car and set off on the next leg of the journey. The car smelled fresh – chemical fresh – and we had to open all the windows, but it was clean and white and ours for the next few weeks.

We left the airport and, carefully following our Google map directions, we booted down the road. Soon, we were zooming down the Calder Freeway for Bendigo, 136 kilometres northwest of Melbourne. The countryside was opening out in front of us. Oh, I can tell you for nothing it felt mighty good to be off that plane.

The lush green of the landscape changed to the browns of the Australian bush. Gum trees and bushes lined the roadside, vast acres of land stretched into the distance, and dried river creeks snuck under the road from time to time. I dozed off to the purr of the engine.

Sometime later, I woke as Granny rounded a corner and beeped the horn. Ahead, I spied a group of people getting out of cars at a great rate. I wondered what all the excitement was about, then I saw what they were all gaping at.

"Granny! Granny, stop the car!"

"What's wrong, Emily?" she asked as she swung the car into the edge at speed and slammed on the brakes.

"Look, Granny! Look over there," I said, pointing to a high bank beside the road.

"Where?"

"Over there, Granny. Can you see him?"

"See what?"

"The koala. Oh dear, he's fallen down again."

I jumped out of the car and rushed over to where the crowd was gathering around the creature. The koala was valiantly trying to climb a steep bank and, as he attempted to grip the bank with his claws, he gnawed the earth with his teeth. He was ever so cute, but mighty skinny.

"I wonder what's wrong with him?" somebody said, examining him minutely. Nobody answered. Everyone just continued gazing at the little guy.

"He's hungry," I said. "He's eating the earth because he can't reach the leaves."

"And they only eat certain types of gum leaves," someone else commented in the background.

"He must have fallen out of that tree above us," another person added, but nobody moved to help.

"Yes," I said, moving towards the scrawny creature, "and he needs to go back into the tree."

But nobody moved. "If doesn't get some gum leaves to eat, he'll die of hunger," I added, looking around me.

Everybody nodded but nobody did anything.

"It's rare to see a koala in the wild." I heard someone mutter into their chest. "They're usually such shy creatures."

Still nobody moved to rescue the little fellow in distress.

"He needs help because he can't climb up the bank by himself," I said, raising my voice and hoping somebody would do something.

Everybody agreed but there was still no action.

"He's old. He can't climb up the bank. He needs help," I said, raising my voice even louder.

This still fetched no reaction. 'How dumb adults can be,' I thought.

"Now," I said in a really loud voice. I looked appealingly at Granny. "Do you think anybody would have a towel in the car?"

At last there was a shuffle and somebody produced a towel.

"Thanks," I said, as Granny helped me to wrap the poor old koala up in the towel so he couldn't scratch us or bite us.

"Now, old boy," I said, as I caught him under his arms. "One, two, three, and up you go."

I threw him as high as I could up on top of the bank. There was a cheer from his audience as he landed half way up the bank and managed to scramble to the top. He turned around, gave a curt little nod and ambled off into the bushes.

I jumped back into the car. "That was amazing," I said.

"Our first encounter with the Australian bush," commented Granny as she climbed into the driver's seat. "A good omen."

'Yes, a very good omen,' I thought, as we set off again, each minute bringing us closer to Rainbow End and my nugget of gold.

CHAPTER 8
HOTEL SHAMROCK

"Granny, just look at that," I said pointing at the hotel. "It's so cool." I couldn't believe we were going to stay in such a grand spot.

"Pa's treat," said Granny smiling. "He mentioned The Shamrock in his letter, so I decided we'd stay here. I suppose we might try our hand at a bit of dancing, too."

"I'd say it's very expensive," I remarked.

"I'd say you're right," said Granny, "but Pa left me property, remember?"

I loved Granny's extravagant gestures. "I hope we're on the second floor," I said, looking up at the balcony, admiringly.

"The Rosalind Suite, no less," she replied with a twinkle, "which overlooks the fountain and the park."

"Oh Granny, this is fab," I said.

We parked in the underground car park around the corner and wheeled our luggage around to the front.

It was a beautiful, old-fashioned building. Granny told me it was an Italianate building and she asked me if I liked the stucco decoration. I wasn't exactly sure what that was, but since I liked everything, I assured her that I did. She smiled for some reason, and told me that the Hotel Shamrock was built in 1854 and it was such an old place that the Bendigo Historical Society used to bring tourists around the building each Sunday.

We walked in the front door and the janitor collected our bags and brought them upstairs. I loved the room. It had high ceilings and felt so spacious. There was a big queen-sized bed for Gran and a lovely, comfy, single bed for me.

Granny must have liked her bed too as she decided to go for a rest. After the long drive and the flight, she was exhausted and she was sound asleep within five minutes. Of course, I was fresh after my snooze in the car, so I decided to go exploring.

I discovered there were two places for dining: the Shamrock Café and Bar for ordinary people, and the fancy Victoria Wine Room upstairs for the VIPs. The Gold Dust

Lounge in the basement was closed until the weekend, and I was just about to go into the Shamrock Sports Bar when I heard a voice behind me.

"Excuse me, young lady."

I turned around.

"You're not allowed into the lounge in the evening."

I stopped, rather nonplussed. "But I'm staying here."

"I know that, but it's the law. Where's your mom?"

"I'm with my granny," I replied, locating the voice behind the counter.

"And where is she?" the voice enquired.

"She went for a rest upstairs," I said. "We've just come from Ireland and she's exhausted.

"From Ireland?" said the voice, and out from behind the high counter emerged a lady in a tight suit.

"Yes."

"That's a long way away. What brought you to Bendigo?"

"Property and gold," I replied. "Why can't I go into the sports bar?"

"Property and gold?" she said. "That sounds interesting."

It suddenly dawned on me that I wasn't going to get very far with this lady unless I gave her the full details. So I said, "Yes, my granny inherited property in Back Creek and I inherited a nugget of gold. Now may I go in?"

"A nugget of gold?"

"From my great-grandfather,"

"And who, pray, was your great-grandfather?"

"His name was Pa O'Neill." The lady's eyes opened wide.

"Hmm... I don't suppose he'd be a Patrick O'Neill, from Cork?"

"Did you know him?" I asked.

"I didn't know him," she replied. "But I might have known of him. Is he still alive?"

"No, he died when I was a baby."

"That's a pity, God rest him."

"Why so?" I asked.

"Well," she said, "my own grandpa is still alive and if Patrick O'Neill is the same man I'm thinking he is, then he was one of my grandpa's best friends."

"Oh," I said, forgetting all about the sports bar and the thousands of TV screens I'd seen inside the door. "By any chance, would your grandpa be called Matt?" This time it was her turn to look surprised.

"How did you know his name?"

So I told the lady all about the letter and the will.

"And he mentioned my grandfather in the letter?" she said, "That's amazing."

"Well, I think it's amazing that you're working in the same hotel where we're staying."

"Oh, that's not a bit strange. I got the job because my grandfather Matt was the local fiddler at the Shamrock all his life."

"And we're staying here because this hotel was mentioned in the letter. Makes sense."

"You know," the lady said, "you're one lucky little girl."

"Well, I would be if I found the gold," I said, "but that's gone missing."

"That'll turn up," she said, turning to greet some Chinese guests who were approaching her counter.

"Perhaps we might go to visit your grandpa?" I suggested.

"Sure," she replied, her attention drawn to the new people. "I'll catch you later."

And I had to be satisfied with that for the present. But in my mind, I decided I was going to hold her to her promise, and I was going to visit Matt Henson. Yes, I was definitely going to meet this old fiddler and I was going to discover all about my great-grandfather Pa O'Neill. And I sped up the stairs as fast as I could to tell Gran my news.

CHAPTER 9
PROSPECTING FOR GOLD

The following morning, we rose at seven and ate an enormous breakfast of bacon and eggs before setting off to find Rainbow End. Gran had only a very sketchy recollection of the place, so I Googled Back Creek, Bendigo, Victoria, and printed off a map with directions. Today was the day I was going to find that nugget of gold that Pa had promised me.

Gran drove ridiculously slowly, but eventually we reached Back Creek. Her excitement was infectious, especially when we stopped at the little bridge and suddenly she recognised the home of her youth.

"Oh!" she said, in wonder. "There's water in the creek for a change. And look over there," she said, pointing to a ridge of rocks. "That's where I used to watch the kangaroos and wallabies coming down to drink."

She parked the car and I was out in a second and bounding down the hill to the creek, and I can tell you that Granny wasn't far behind me.

"That's the place where I caught my first fish," she said pointing to a curve in the stream. "There was a huge flood one winter, and when the water receded, an enormous fish got trapped in that pool. Pa helped me catch it with a net he had for straining the butter. We had such a great time."

"Does it look the same?" I asked.

"It's just as I remembered it, only smaller," she said, picking up an old pan in the bushes. "One of Pa's friends showed me how to pan for gold, and I spent many lazy hours panning for gold with this pan in that corner over there."

"And did you ever strike lucky?" I asked.

"Not a chance," she replied, "but I had a lot of fun in the process."

"And where was your favourite place, Granny?" I asked, getting a little bit impatient.

"Oh, Emily," she teased. "I wonder is it my favourite place or your nugget of gold you're asking about?"

"Your favourite place, of course Granny," I replied, "but I suppose it might be interesting to find the nugget of gold too... The one that we've travelled thousands of miles to find!"

Granny laughed as she led me down a little dust track beside the creek to the bridge, close to where we'd parked the car.

"Here it is," she said, directing my gaze to another outcrop of rock beside the bridge. "My favourite spot as a child. This is where I used to play mummies and daddies. My baby used to be a woollen dolly my mam made me. That's where I put the cot," she said, pointing to a hollow, "and the table was up on that ledge. And guess what? I used to make meals out of kangaroo poop mixed with water and dust from the creek."

"That's disgusting," I said.

"And then I used to decorate the meal with gum leaves and twigs." Granny laughed. "We only pretended to eat the gorgeous meals, you know."

"That's still disgusting," I said. "Anyway, Granny, the nugget... Where did you hide the nugget?"

"Oh," she said, scratching her head. "Now where was it that I used to put it?"

"Ah, Granny, come on now. Tell me where you put it."

Suddenly she became quite serious. "It mightn't be there, you know. Pa might have put it somewhere else for safe keeping."

"I know, but we might as well have a look anyway," I said, pretending not to be too excited.

Gran showed me a tiny hole in the rickety wall of the bridge. Then she carefully lifted out a stone that was blocking the hole and slipped her hand behind an outcrop of rock that was jutting out.

"I can't reach it. Perhaps Pa poked it in with a stick. Your hands are smaller. You try."

I slipped my hand in. I could feel the hole going along the back of the rock. I stretched my arm along the crevice and my fingertips felt a bit of cloth. I caught the cloth in between my first two fingers and gently eased out the piece. I was shaking and I thought Gran was going to have a heart attack. Out came this big long bit of red rag.

"It's in the rag," I shouted, but all that came out of the rag was a few stones.

"I'm afraid not," Gran said. "That was my rag money. Try again."

I slipped my hand back in until it reached the end of the hole.

"There's nothing there," I said. "It's not there. The nugget of gold is not in the hole."

"Are you sure?" asked Granny, pulling at the rocks.

"I'm positive," I said. "It's definitely not there." And suddenly, all the excitement fell out of me and this great, big wave of disappointment rolled into its place. Now, I'd never be able to help Gran with our debts. It just wasn't fair.

Granny kept scraping away at the boulders until she had dragged the last rock out, "I was so sure it would be there. I'm so sorry, Emily."

My lip began to tremble and then I must admit I started to cry.

"It's definitely not there," I grunted. I don't usually cry, but I really thought that all I had to do was go to Granny's favourite spot and the nugget of gold would be waiting for me. How stupid can you get?

"All is not lost," said Granny. "Perhaps the gold is in the bank. Perhaps Pa put the nugget in the bank for safekeeping. Perhaps nuggets of gold are kept in a special place in Australia. We'll call into the bank tomorrow and find out. In the meantime," she said, turning around,

"Look up there to the left, in the circle of trees. Can you see anything?"

I looked up to the left and there, hidden in the trees, I caught a glimpse of a house.

"Is that Rainbow End?" I asked, perking up a bit.

"That's it," said Gran. "Come, we'll see if it's still the way I remember it," and Granny set off up the hill at a quick pace, with me scampering as fast as I could after her.

The speed these grannies can travel would surprise you sometimes!

CHAPTER 10
DISCOVERING THE JOURNAL

The house had almost completely fallen down. The tin roof over the timber shingles was half caved in, and the remnants of curtains blew lazily out through the empty frames. A wooden fence surrounding the house had cracked down and was rotting back into the ground, and I could see a rusty bike thrown up against one of the posts.

"Come on," said Gran. "I'll show you."

We climbed up through the bushes until we came to the tumbledown shack. A battered door hung crookedly on bent hinges. All the furniture was thrown around the place and it smelled of dead animal.

I looked at Granny. She was frowning, disappointment written all over her face.

"Congratulations. Nice house, Gran," I said wickedly, beginning to see the funny side of things. "What a splendid property you've inherited."

Granny cast a look in my direction and if looks could kill, I was dead.

"Aren't we the lucky people," I added for good measure. "Me with the phantom nugget and you with the exotic palace!" Gran's lip began to quiver and then, thankfully, she burst out laughing.

"You're a rogue," Gran said, wiping the tears from her eyes and becoming solemn. "It may not be the place I remember, but this is where I was born. Show a little respect."

She beckoned me in. "Come along, my dear, and let's meet the ghosts of yesteryear."

The two of us wandered through the doorway and surveyed our surroundings. It had been completely ransacked, but an old stove was still there in the corner with a few pots and pans strewn across it. A rough table was jammed up underneath the window and two broken chairs lay on the floor.

"Either the ghosts or the neighbours aren't too friendly," I commented.

We went into the tiny bedroom beside the kitchen. An iron bed sat in the middle of the room. The mattress was completely destroyed, and a moth-eaten quilt lay discarded on the floor. A few items of clothing hung on pegs and a rickety lamp had fallen to the ground.

"Looks rather sad, doesn't it?" said Gran. "You know, this is probably the room where I was actually born." She moved over to the window and fingered the torn floral wallpaper.

"This used to be pretty once upon a time," she said, softly, "but time moves on."

She moved to the sideboard beside the window and rubbed her fingers along the dusty rim of wood. The drawers, packed with an assortment of rubbish, dangled at lopsided angles from the old piece of furniture.

"And I remember this sideboard used to be my mother's pride and joy," she said, closing the drawers one by one. "It was here when they bought the cottage. Apparently, it was made by one of the early pioneers. I always felt it was such a homely piece."

She pushed the last drawer into place and, as she rattled the drawer, a corner of a book appeared. It had become dislodged and was peeping out of its hiding spot.

"What's this, I wonder?" I said, pulling the book out. Sandwiched between the underside of the drawer and the base of the sideboard, it had remained hidden for years.

"The detective in action again, I see," said Granny, wryly.

The hard cover of the book was ripped in places. The pages were yellow with age and inside the cover was a picture of an old fashioned girl in a black dress, and pages of beautifully-formed handwriting.

I turned to the front page and there on top were the words 'My Journal, by Tessie Bryan', with the date 29th March 1859.

"Granny," I cried. "It's a diary written nearly 150 years ago. Wow!"

"My goodness, this is a very different type of treasure," said Gran as she took the journal from me and examined it carefully. "You know, Emily, you may not have found that nugget of gold today, but you certainly found something very precious."

"I wonder if there's anything else there," I said, rummaging about underneath the drawer, but nothing was forthcoming.

Granny handed me back the book. "It's time to go. In Australia, darkness falls very quickly and the lights on my car aren't the best. You can read the journal back at the hotel."

Oh, the frustration! But what could I do? I had a journal that I couldn't read until we got back to the hotel, and my nugget of gold was still missing.

CHAPTER 11
THE GOLD RUSH

Back at the hotel, I snuck up the stairs, snuggled under the duvet and began to read. Apart from a pit stop and a drink, I didn't stop until I had read the entire journal. But it was worth reading because, guess what? Hidden in the story about Tessie was the next clue to finding my nugget.

29th March 1859

I'm Tessie Bryan. Today is my birthday and I'm twelve years of age. It is the most memorable day of my life because today I set foot on Australian soil for the first time. You have no idea how incredible it felt to walk on firm ground after months aboard the Edwin Fox. And, as a special treat for my birthday, my father bought me this journal. I've never owned a real book before. At home in Carrigtwohill, we used to write with chalk on little blackboards at school, but now I've got my very own journal and I'm going to write in it every day.

Melbourne is a fine town full of brick buildings, and there's also a place close by called Canvas Town, because it's full of tents. Tomorrow, we're going shopping there for provisions, but today we're relaxing after the long journey from Ireland. We're staying in The Lamb's Inn overlooking the Yarra Yarra River, and Papa has promised Mam and me a real hot bath in the tub. I can't wait.

30th March

We went to Canvas Town and Papa bought a wooden wagon with a canvas hood, and a horse that I've called Winkie because he has only one eye. He also bought tackle and oats for the horse and potatoes and meat for us. He says everything costs a fortune here.

Oh yes, he bought boards of timber too, and you may well ask why.

I must explain that Papa is a carpenter by trade. He used to work on Lord Barrymore's Estate. That was before the police discovered that he was a member of the Whiteboys, and we had to leave at speed in the middle of the night, but that's another story. Mam and I were left in charge of buying food for the journey and bits and bobs for our new house. We'll be off soon.

31st March

Tomorrow we're heading off for Sandhurst, which everybody nicknames the Big Gold Mountain. It might take up to a week to get there, as the roads are bad after all the rain. I hope the wagon doesn't get stuck in any potholes.

The weather here is cool but the rain has stopped so we should have a good journey. Everybody tells us that we have come at the right time of the year, as the weather can be impossibly hot sometimes. Things are upside down here. Winter is in summer and summer is in winter. I think it's because we are at the other side of the equator now.

1st April

We got up early and packed the wagon. Apart from the food, it was full of nails, hinges, carpenter tools and panning equipment. Papa has got the gold fever. He says his money will just stretch to buying a patch of land, but we'll have to find some gold to get our business up and running. There's a big trail of wagons travelling together to Sandhurst because it's dangerous to travel alone. There are bushrangers and vagabonds living up in the hills and, if you travel alone, they're likely to come down in hordes and steal your belongings. Papa hasn't got a gun but a lot of the men have them.

2nd April

Last night, I saw some dark coloured children down at the water hole where we camped. I had blisters on my feet from all the walking and, when I went down to bathe them in the water, I saw the black fellows. They only wore loincloths and they were playing in the sand, but when they saw me, they ran away.

Mam says they're afraid of us because white people treat them the same way in Australia as the landlords treat poor spailpín people in Ireland.

3rd April

I made a friend today called Bob. We met around the campfire. He's great fun. His family have a flock of sheep. They're butchers. Bob says that gold diggers need to eat so their family aim to become the premier butchers in Sandhurst.

4th April

Today, I saw kangaroos, wallabies and koalas. The kangaroos look like deer, but they sit back on their powerful back legs and hop along with their paws suspended up in the air. The wallabies look just like them but they are smaller.

The koalas are the best. They look like cuddly little bears with pudgy noses. They live high up in the gum trees and spend their entire lives eating the gum leaves.

It's at dusk when the animals seem to come out.

At the moment, we're camped in a forest. Everybody is anxious in case the raiders come. One man sounded the alarm half an hour ago but it only turned out to be a kangaroo.

5th April

The raiders came last night. We were so scared. Mam and I were asleep in the wagon and Papa was sleeping underneath. They had horses and guns and they rode into the middle of the camp screaming at us to hand over our *money. I thought it was all over for us, but then we heard rifle shots in the distance and, before you could wink, the raiders had disappeared into the night again.*

We were so lucky. The man who had sounded the false alarm yesterday had dispatched a message to Sandhurst saying that we were being attacked, so a posse of police had been sent out to protect us. Thank goodness for that kangaroo!

6th April

The wheel nearly came off today. Poor old Winkie had to get off the track quickly when the coach carrying passengers, gold and mail from Sandhurst to Melbourne passed by. The coach was travelling at a ferocious speed and it was closely guarded by police who made everybody scarper out of the way. By the time they'd passed, our wagon had become firmly stuck in a deep rut by the side of the road. If it hadn't been for Bob's family helping us out, we'd be stuck yet.

I clambered out of bed and stretched. It was strange reading about a girl like me, a century and a half ago. I opened my bottle of water and had a drink. Everything was so new for the people who came to Australia then. Imagine not knowing what a kangaroo looked like!

I wandered into the bathroom, did my business and, as I looked in the mirror, it struck me that I'd like to actually touch a kangaroo when I was in Australia. I'd never done that before, so maybe Tessie and I weren't so very different. Just the new experiences in Australia were different.

Back to bed I went again, pulled the duvet around my ears and continued to read.

CHAPTER 12
THE EARLY SETTLERS

7th April

We finally arrived in Sandhurst. The whole town is like a sea of tents, but there are a few brick buildings and a few buildings made out of wood and stone. After the scare we had on the journey, Papa made it his business to go straight to the Bendigo Building Society and lodge his money. Then he went off to Camp Hill to get a miner's licence and see if there was any land for sale. He was looking for a place in Sandhurst but somebody told him that the drinking water in Sandhurst was all polluted by the gold panning, so they suggested we might buy a place along Back Creek.

We're going to see that tomorrow, but today we're going to set up our tent and Mam and I are going shopping.

8th April

The fashions here are interesting.

The women wear big hoop skirts that flounce around the place and they go up and down the street with their baskets. The men wear white linen coats and trousers, and either light coloured felt hats or funny headgear made out of some plaited fibre.

You'd hear all sorts of languages here, as well. Most of the diggers come from China but there are people from Germany, France, England, Scotland, Wales and Ireland here too. The first gold was found about eight years ago, and now the place is swarming with people searching for it. The alluvial gold seems to have gone, and now people are beginning to dig mine shafts looking for gold-bearing reefs.

9th April

We went to see the property in Back Creek. It's a long way out from Sandhurst, but at least we'll be able to get fresh water, and Papa says he can ride Winkie into town to go to work.

Bob is going to live just outside the town, so he says his family are going to join the new Bendigo Agricultural and Horticultural Society. Papa says we can have our own society at home, grow our own vegetables and keep a few sheep and hens.

10th April

Papa bought the place. We're calling it Rainbow End and we're going to live there soon. Papa says he's going to build a sandstone house with timber shingles on the roof. He says he's going to build Mam a veranda and there's going to be stone paving on the floor. Mam has also decided where she's going to put the new sideboard he's promised her. I wonder will he put false bottoms into the drawers. The folk in the big house in Ireland always asked him to put them in.

11th April

We went to church today in the new Wesleyan Methodist Church at Golden Square. Everybody calls it 'Jimmy Jeffrey's Church', because Jimmy was one of the first diggers to come to Sandhurst in 1852, and he used to preach on a tree stump nearby.

12th April

It's our last day in Sandhurst, so Mam and I are going to a new shop that has just opened and we're going to buy tableware and other utensils for our new house. Papa is calling into George Fletcher to see if he can do the woodwork for the Town Hall that he's designing.

Everything is new here and there's great talk about the eight reservoirs along the Bendigo Valley that Joseph Brady is designing to bring fresh water to the town. I love living here. Mind you, everybody is telling us that we'll hate it when the hot weather arrives, and we'll be eaten alive by mosquitoes and flies.

13th April

We started our house. Papa is going to build a kitchen and a bedroom straightaway, and when we're rich he'll build a parlour and another little bedroom for me. In the meantime, I can sleep on the settle in the kitchen. I've a bit of a headache. I hope it will be better soon as I want to go into town with Papa later on.

14th April

I'm stuck at home. I've still got the headache and I'm feeling feverish. I think I'll lie down for a while. Will write tomorrow.

15th April

Today, I feel absolutely miserable. I feel weak and every part of me aches. My dreadful headache is worse and my tummy hurts. I can't eat.

16th April

No better today. Papa has gone for the doctor. I'm very feverish and cold at the same time. There's a red rash on my body.

17 April

The doctor says I'm bad with scarlatina. Can't move... Can't write... Just too tired... Sorry, Journal.

And underneath the last entry, written in completely different handwriting, were these terrible words:

Tess Bryan died from scarlatina on 19th April 1859, aged twelve years.

I put the journal down just as Gran came into the room. I couldn't believe that Tess's life had just been snuffed out. I looked up.

"She died," I said. "She was my age."

Granny came over and sat on the corner of the bed. "I'm sorry to hear that."

"Why did she die, Granny?" I asked. It was such a surprise at the end of the journal, such a nasty, nasty surprise.

"A lot of children died young in those days," she replied, rubbing my hand. "The wonder drug, penicillin, wasn't invented then."

"She died of scarlatina. She didn't even last a month here," I continued, a sense of shock building up inside me.

"Times were tough, and many people died on the ships before they got to Australia."

"But she made it," I said.

"Yes, Emily, but these things happened. Her immune system was probably weakened by all the travelling and the bad conditions."

Realising that I was about to start crying, Granny changed the subject.

"What else did you discover about poor Tessie?" she asked, turning the pages.

"Well," I said, trying not to think of Tess dying, "she wrote that her father was a carpenter and that he'd promised his wife he'd build her a sideboard, and Tess was wondering if her dad would make the drawers with false bottoms."

"Hmm..." said Gran. "Secret drawers. That sounds interesting."

"Secret drawers...?" I said, perking up. "I just thought the false bottoms were the spaces underneath the drawers where Tessie hid her journal."

"Oh, no," said Gran. "False bottoms were the name for secret compartments in the old days."

I blinked. "So you think we might find things in the false bottoms?"

"Possibly," said Granny winking at me. "Long ago, carpenters were highly-skilled craftsmen and were often asked to make these compartments for rich people to hide their money."

"Oh Granny," I whispered. "Perhaps Pa found the secret drawer and put the nugget in it."

"Perhaps," she replied. "There's a possibility… a slim possibility."

"But one that deserves investigation!" I said. "We'll definitely have to go to Rainbow End tomorrow!"

"I'm afraid not," Granny replied. "Tomorrow, we're going sight seeing in Bendigo and I have to make an appointment to visit the lawyer and sort out the deeds for Rainbow End."

"And we can go after that?"

"Then, we're going to the bank to see if Pa lodged the nugget."

"Oh," I said, knowing for certain in my head exactly where my nugget was hiding. "And afterwards, we can go to Rainbow End?"

"My goodness, you are persistent," Granny replied, laughing, "Afterwards, we'll go to bed. If the nugget has remained safely in the secret drawer for the last number of years, I'm guessing that it will remain safely there for another day or so."

And I had to be satisfied. Children have to accept adult decisions – one of life's golden rules!

CHAPTER 13
DEBORAH MINE

The following morning, we went exploring Bendigo. I badly wanted to go out to Rainbow End, but Granny said she had a great desire to visit all the local places that Pa and Nan would have known in 1945. She said she wanted to get 'a feel for the place'.

Across the road from our hotel was this elegant old building called Bendigo Visitor Centre, so Gran said we'd go in and discover all about the local tourist attractions.

She got brochures and one of the ladies who worked there told her that we were very lucky to be in town because the Chinese Easter Festival was at the weekend, but that, in the mean time, we should definitely visit the Deborah Mine.

I pricked up my ears. This was the very mine mentioned in the letter. The place where Pa worked and from where he was meant to have stolen some gold. Suddenly, it struck me that somebody might remember him. Somebody might know something about Pa. Maybe this sightseeing wasn't such a bad idea.

"Let's go, Gran," I said, picking up the leaflets. "Our next stop!"

We arrived at 9.30am, bang on time for the Mine Experience Tour. We paid our money, donned our hard hats and miners' lamps and trundled out to where the tour began at the poppet head.

Ahead of us were two families. In the first family, there was a mum, a dad and two nicely polished up children in their denim skirts, white tee shirts, neatly-tied ponytails and pink flip-flops. In the second family, there was a mum with a whining child dangling on her hip and a harassed dad chasing two wild boys who kept climbing up on everything. He would drag them off and tell them to be good, and they would climb back up again and laugh down at him.

But guess who joined us right as the tour was about to begin? You're right. It was the maggot and his mother. And, surprisingly enough, I was delighted to see him. Given the company we had, I thought a bit of intelligence wouldn't go astray.

"I didn't get your name the last time?" I said in a friendly way.

"No," he said.

"So what is it?" I asked.

"Bill," he said. "Bill Bates." And then he turned away. He obviously presumed I had no more Werther's.

'How friendly,' I thought, as I heard the tour begin.

"Central Deborah Mine," the guide said, "was opened in 1939 and closed in 1954, the year Queen Elizabeth visited Bendigo. It was a very short period of time, but, during that era, the mine produced about 929 kilograms of gold." He paused for effect, "worth about 8 billion in today's terms."

We all looked suitably impressed, except for the two lads who were being dragged off the poppet head.

For those of you who don't know, the poppet head looks like the Eiffel Tower with the top knocked off.

"And today," the guide continued, "Central Deborah Mine shares its rich history with thousands of visitors each year.

"Of course, gold was discovered in Bendigo much earlier than 1939. A lady called Margaret discovered some alluvial gold in 1851, when she was washing her laundry in the river at Ravenswood Sheep Run. And, as soon as the news spread, people flocked here. And did you know," he said, peering at us, "that mining became so important that at one time there were 5,600 gold mines in Bendigo?"

The guide stopped for a breath as he waited for the dad to retrieve the two boys who had run off into the blacksmith's shop. When the dad returned a few moments later holding a child by each hand, the guide continued.

"That cage," he said, pointing to the small box structure under the poppet head, "was used not only to transport miners above and below ground but also to haul rock, or ore, to the surface to be processed."

He paused again. "Can you imagine going down 17 levels? Down 412 metres in a tiny cage, into a black hole?" The girls shook their heads.

Of course, the boys didn't answer at all, because they had escaped from Dad and were already in the cage and rattling it furiously.

The guide waited patiently as the dad disengaged the boys' hands from the grill around the cage and pulled them out of it.

"Today," he said, "we won't be going down in this cage. We have an easier route, and you'll be glad to know we're only going down 61 metres. Follow me."

And he led the way to a large shaft opening into the mine. He explained how the tunnel roof was kept from collapsing over the years and he explained all the safety features. Bates kept heckling him for more information, so we got great value for money.

The first place we visited when we went down in the elevator was the crib. This was where the miners ate. It used to take forever to go up and down in the tiny cage, so the miners all ate underground. Originally, they used candles. These were later replaced by acetylene gas lamps and finally by battery operated lamps.

"But," said the guide, "just to get the feel of how dark it actually is down here, we'll all turn off our lamps at the count of three. And," he added, "I want you to wave your hand in front of your face and see what happens. All ready? One, two, three..." And we all switched off our lamps.

Next thing, we heard two piercing screams, followed by loud bawling. We turned on our lamps and discovered the two brats with their mouths wide open roaring as loudly as they could.

"Somebody slapped me," roared one.

"Somebody hit me," screamed the other. The noise was deafening.

"Shut up," shouted Bates at the top of his voice. "Shut up, shut up, and shut up." And then the baby joined in, and she succeeded in being the loudest of them all. It was bedlam. But that wasn't all. The little girls sidled up to their concerned parents and, in the next minute, the mother with the baby rounded on me.

"How dare you? How dare you hit my children?" she screamed at me.

I was stunned. I could say nothing. Then Granny joined in the fracas.

"Excuse me," she said. "How dare you speak to my granddaughter in this manner?"

Next minute, the mad woman started heading in my direction. I was wondering what was going to happen when the guide intervened.

"Calm down everybody. It was just an accident, the lassie just couldn't see in the dark."

"But I didn't do it," I protested.

"Don't worry at all about it," said the guide patting me on the shoulder. "It could happen to a saint."

"I didn't do it," I muttered, but nobody seemed to be listening. The respectable family were speaking quietly amongst themselves, Bates' mother was telling her son not to be upset, the dad of the crying boys was consoling them, the guide was trying to distract the squealing baby, and my Granny was standing in front of me, facing the mad woman, and telling her in a very firm voice that if she controlled her children, there wouldn't be a problem.

Me, I just watched the spectacle. What was the point in arguing?

After a while, the brats stopped roaring and the tour continued. We were shown the little nodules of gold found along the seams of the rock face, and the pyrite, which glistened like gold but had little value. The guide also showed us different mining techniques and how the explosives were used. I learned heaps.

Of course, by this stage, the boys were fully recovered and back to their usual antics. They were so naughty. I could see by Granny's pursed lips that she wasn't amused, especially when they raced up and down the tunnels like maniacs.

Then we met an old miner. I wondered if he'd have known Pa. He looked about ninety years of age, but I'm not good at guessing people's ages.

He told us about his work down the mine and he showed us a stick with a screw top. He explained how miners sometimes used to smuggle gold out of the mine in the hole underneath the screw top. I glanced over at Granny, who was listening intently. The miner definitely must have known Pa. I put up my hand to ask him if he had ever heard of Patrick O'Neill, when the guide spoke.

"Excuse me, sir," he said turning to the brats' father. "Do you know the whereabouts of your children?"

We all looked around. There was no sign of them anywhere. We stopped talking and listened but there wasn't a sound. Then their parents started calling out their names, but not a murmur was heard from the boys. The parents waved their hands frantically. They shouted louder, but there was still no response. Granny and I joined in the chorus and soon everybody was calling out for the boys simultaneously, except for the maggot. He was bending over, holding his hands over his ears and telling everyone that the noise hurt his head. Still, there was no reply from the boys.

The old miner whispered something to the guide, and the guide motioned us all to be quiet.

"The boys can't have gone far. We'll split up. You," he said, pointing to Granny, Bates, his mum, and myself, "will go with Mikey down that passage and the rest of us will go this way. Remember, there is no mobile coverage down the mine, so stick together."

Without delay, we lined up behind Mikey the miner and headed down the shaft into the darkness.

CHAPTER 14
THE GHOST

The old miner hobbled along with his stick. Every now and again he would stop, give a loud holler, listen intently and move on. He growled in a low voice and his comments about the boys rumbled down the shaft. Somehow, it didn't seem the right time to ask him about Pa.

Bates' mother and Granny were directly behind the miner, and the two of us were bringing up the rear. Bates was just ahead of me and he was getting slower and slower. The gap between our parents and us was widening. When I told him to hurry up, he got stubborn.

"I'm going as fast as I can," he said.

"Well try harder or we'll be left behind," I muttered.

He huffed and puffed and deliberately slowed up.

"Go on ahead, if you like," he said. "I'm not stopping you."

"Can't you see that if we don't keep up, we'll get lost ourselves?"

He was beginning to irritate me. Then he stopped altogether.

"The girls did it," he announced.

"Did what?" I asked.

"The two girls hit the boys."

"What?" I said. "How do you know?"

"I heard them talking about it."

"And why did you let me get blamed for it?" I asked.

"Everyone was shouting and my head hurt," he replied.

"That mad woman nearly hit me."

"My head hurt," he said defensively. I spun around and barely prevented myself from punching him.

"What is wrong with you?" I asked. "In some ways you're so smart and in other ways you're just not with it. What is wrong with you?" I repeated.

There was silence. He debated for a minute and I thought he was going to explain himself, but then he shook himself. "There's nothing wrong with me."

"Then you'd better get your act together and get walking," I said, "because the others have disappeared and I can barely hear them anymore."

He turned around and continued up along the tunnel. That idiot knew I didn't slap the boys and yet he did nothing about it. My mind was so bubbling with fury that I never noticed that we had come to a fork in the tunnel. We had obviously taken the wrong route and I suddenly realised that we could no longer hear the others in the distance.

"Stop," I said. "We've taken a wrong turn. We have to go back."

Bates stopped. "I'm not going back. The others are just around the corner."

"No, they aren't."

"I can hear them," he said blithely.

"Well, I can't hear anything," I said listening keenly. "Are you sure?"

"There's another fork to the right here and if we go this way, we'll meet up with the others. It's a shortcut," he said.

"Are you positive you can hear them?" I enquired again.

"Yes," he said as he turned down to the right.

I didn't know what to do. I gave a few hollers myself but there was no response and by this stage Bates was rapidly disappearing from view down the tunnel. It was decision time, and I decided that I'd prefer to have company if I was lost so I rushed down after Bates.

"I hope you're right," I muttered. There was no response. We walked and walked and the darkness and the silence seemed to get deeper and deeper. Finally, I grabbed the back of his jacket.

"Stop," I said. "We're lost."

"I know," he replied, shrugging me off.

I gritted my teeth. "Then why didn't you stop earlier?"

"Because if we keep going right we'll eventually get back to where we started," he announced.

"No, we won't," I said, "the mine isn't laid out in a grid. It's not a town. Miners follow gold reefs and they don't go in straight lines."

"Well, I'm going on," he said, "You can do what you like."

I looked at him in amazement. What do you do when you know somebody is absolutely wrong and you're not in a position to do anything about it? I had to think quickly.

"Wait," I ordered. "I need a rest." That seemed to work. I sat down.

"What's your phone number?" I asked.

"It doesn't work down here," he replied.

"Well, give it to me anyway," I said, trying to buy a bit of time. He reluctantly gave me his number. Then I was stumped. How would I delay him? Suddenly I thought of the mine story.

"Did you ever hear of Lady Deborah?"

"What about her?" he asked.

"Well this mine is named after her," I replied.

"I know," he said, "but you're going to tell me about her anyway."

"Yes," I replied tartly, "I found her story on the internet."

I rummaged in my pocket. "Now where is it?" I said, fishing for the scrap of paper where I had written it down. I opened the sheet and began to read in my elocution voice.

"Many years ago, a penniless English lord emigrated to Australia to make his fortune in the gold mines. His drunken brother had squandered the family fortune, and the lord wished to reclaim the estate with his newfound wealth.

"Can you remember if the estate was in Ireland or England?"

"I'm not sure. It doesn't matter." I turned up my lamp. "Finally, he arrived in Bendigo."

"Sandhurst," Bates corrected.

"He arrived in Sandhurst," I read, squinting at the writing in the dim light, "and he set about making his fortune. He was convinced that a rich quartz reef of gold lay hidden under the town, and it became an obsession with him to find this reef. He made a few minor strikes, but he failed to find the gold reef of his dreams.

"One day the Lola Montez chorus line came to town to entertain the miners, and the young lord fell madly in love with Deborah, one of the dancers."

"Such fiction!" Bates sneered.

"It's a legend," I replied, "and you're to stop interrupting."

"Deborah," I continued, "was very beautiful. She had bewitching eyes and a sparkling smile that entranced all who met her. When the lord saw her at the show, her beauty and her charm enchanted him. It was love at first sight. Her winsome ways delighted him and he swore he'd wed her the very day he discovered the elusive reef of gold. To this end, he worked night and day down in the depths of the mine. His health deteriorated and despite his beloved Deborah beseeching him to stop, he continued his search.

"This is boring," said Bates, but I took no notice of him and continued reading my romantic story.

"One bleak day, he failed to return. Deborah was distraught. She begged his fellow miners to descend and search for the missing man. Alas, he was discovered dead, clutching an enormous nugget of gold to his chest and, in the wall where he had been digging, the miners could clearly see the gold reef."

"Are you nearly finished?" Bates asked.

I didn't bother to reply. "Deborah was beside herself with grief and refused to leave the mine. For two days and two nights, she stayed there refusing to eat or drink. And on the second night, she disappeared. Search parties were sent out to look for her but she had completely vanished and no trace of her was ever found again."

Bates yawned, "I'm actually familiar with that story, and I find it tedious. Is that the end?"

"Shush," I ordered and continued. "And, to this day, a mysterious figure walks the mine. The miners call her Lady Deborah. She protects the mine and, whenever somebody is in trouble, she comes to their aid."

Bates deliberately yawned again.

"And legend has it," I continued, "that when a sighting of the mysterious lady is reported, invariably a rich gold strike is imminent." I stopped for dramatic effect.

"Are you ready to go now?" he asked.

I just looked at him. "Are you for real?"

"What do you mean?" he asked.

"Do you ever think of anybody else only yourself? Do you have any feelings at all?"

He didn't reply and I didn't budge. "Well?" I demanded.

"If you must know," he said, "I have a condition."

"Should that explain your behaviour to me?" I asked.

"My brain is not like your brain," he said.

'You can say that again,' I thought, as I waited for him to continue.

Bates paused, "I have a greater capacity to retain knowledge than most people because the region in my brain that stores information is larger and better equipped than it is for other people."

'Lucky you,' I thought.

"But my head," he continued, "is the same size as everybody else's, which means, in effect, that other areas in my brain are smaller."

"The feelings areas," I suggested, suddenly wishing to understand.

Bates looked at the wall. "The psychologist tells me this is one of the reasons why I have difficulties with people."

"Well, perhaps that explains it," I said.

Bates glanced sideways at me. "I have to go to classes to learn how to respond to other people. I find it rather tedious, but I'm told it's necessary."

"They're right," I had it out before I could think.

"What do you mean?" he asked, frowning slightly.

"You're smart, but you mess up around people all the time."

A bewildered Bates scratched his head.

"You're not perfect, which I guess means you're normal... just different."

Bates looked at me and I haven't a clue what went through his head, except he faced down the tunnel and announced. "I'm going."

"You can't," I said, "or we'll get even more lost."

"We're not lost," he replied. "Look, there's a lady with a light at the end of the tunnel."

I looked and, right enough, there was the black outline of a woman holding a lamp. She had a bun piled up on her head. I called her and she looked over her shoulder before moving on. A shiver went down my spine.

"Bates," I said, "There's something very strange about that woman."

Bates made no reply.

"She's the ghost," I whispered.

"Well, she seems to know her way around," he muttered, moving towards her.

We followed her through a maze of tunnels. She didn't appear to be moving quickly, but somehow we never seemed to catch up with her. Finally, we rounded a bend and I spotted Granny. I couldn't believe it.

"Granny, we're here." I screamed, running down the tunnel into her arms. And, a few minutes later, the two boys appeared. They told us that a beautiful lady in old-fashioned clothes had shown them the way back.

"The Lady Deborah herself," the miner said nodding. "Still coming to people's aid. Mark my words, there'll be gold found in the near future."

Bates made no comment.

CHAPTER 15
THE TOURIST TRAIL

After visiting Deborah Mine, the rest of Bendigo seemed very tame. In my mind, I could see Lady Deborah walking ahead of us in the mine, and the miner's prediction kept rattling around in my head. I badly wanted to go straight out to Rainbow End, but Granny thought the excitement about seeing the ghost was a bit of a joke, and she told me, with a chuckle, that Lady Deborah would mind the nugget for us while we went sightseeing.

"So where are we going?" I asked in a miffed voice.

"Everywhere," she replied, producing her list.

It was all very official, and I discovered that Bendigo must have been a very busy place at the end of the 19th century, because the post office, the Law Courts, the Bee Hive Store, Shamrock Hotel, Bendigo Pottery, Bendigo Art Gallery, the Sacred Heart Cathedral, Bendigo Jail, Bendigo Botanical Gardens, St Paul's Anglican Cathedral, the

Bendigo School of Mines and Industries building and the Town Hall were all built at that time.

We walked around the edges of Rosalind Park and saw most of the buildings on the list. Then we branched out to the other places and bought one of Gillies' Aussie Pies.

I was just sinking my teeth into one of these famous pies when I noticed that we were beside the bank.

"Gran," I said. "Look where we are!"

"How fortuitous," she replied, examining the sign. "Well spotted."

We went into the bank, but there was no information about Patrick O'Neill's nugget of gold. I didn't expect any. The manager went online, but apparently there wasn't any nugget registered under Patrick O'Neill's name in any bank.

No surprise there.

Very often, he told us, these nuggets were sold on the black market and ended up in China, and, from there, they were dispersed all over the world. Since I felt certain that I knew where the nugget was hidden, I felt we were wasting time, but Granny was determined to check out the situation.

Afterwards, we did a lot more walking around, and it seemed strange looking at the buildings that Granny's Pa and Mam would have seen. Sometimes, we had a little peek inside and other times we just admired the outsides of the buildings.

We went to the lawyer's office and the prim secretary gave us an appointment to see him first thing the following morning. She was the sort of person who always thinks she is doing the other person a favour. I didn't like her, but job done.

We headed for Bendigo Art Gallery. The gallery was a massive, red-brick building with huge glass panes at the entrance. I guess it looked old and new all at the one time.

Granny likes history, so she wanted to see the 19th-century Australian paintings in the Bolton Court gallery. We went through a white doorway into a red room and, when I saw all the paintings lined up around the walls, I felt I was stepping into the past.

We were just looking at James Meadow's painting 'Sandhurst from Camp Hill 1886', and trying to figure out the differences between the present day streets on our map and the ones in the painting, when the Chinese family from the Shamrock Hotel joined us. The Chans were out sightseeing too and, when they saw what we were doing, Mei Ling, their daughter, helped me with the map while Granny started talking to her parents.

"So, you're coming to live here?" I overheard Gran say.

"Yes," the dad replied. "I've just started work with the mining company in Bendigo, and my family are deciding whether to buy a house in the area or rent one."

Of course, when Granny heard he was looking for a house, she couldn't resist telling them about Rainbow End.

"In Back Creek?" he inquired.

"Oh yes," said Gran, explaining the exact location.

"Back Creek, Bendigo?"

So Gran described the place to him, and he did seem interested... surprisingly interested, I thought, considering it was such a ramshackle place.

After a bit more chatting, he said something in private to his wife before turning to Gran.

"Excuse me," he said, "I must go and attend to some business." Then he shook hands and left.

I thought Mei Ling and her mum would go with him, but they decided they'd come with us instead.

"Well," said Gran smiling at us. "What about going to the Discovery Science and Technology Centre?" So off we all set.

The Centre turned out to be full of fascinating stuff for kids, but the area that Mei Ling and I most wanted to visit was the planetarium. We stretched out on beanbags on a starry blue carpet, gazed into the black ceiling that was lit up by constellations, and chatted while we waited for the talk to begin.

Mei Ling told me that her dad was in charge of purchasing land on behalf of the mining company, and I told her about the search for my nugget of gold. Then, the man came in and we talked about the stars you see in different parts of the world.

In Australia, the Southern Cross (the smallest of the 88 western constellations), can be seen at most times of the year, but people who live in Ireland and Northern China never see it unless they travel south, whereas the southern Australians never see the Big Dipper unless they travel north.

We found out how to find south by using the Southern Cross and the two pointer stars. If you draw a straight line through the long axis of the Southern Cross, and another straight line through the middle of the pointers, where those two lines meet is the South Celestial Pole. And, if you go straight down to the horizon from there, you are heading south. Rather handy.

As we were leaving the room of stars, Mrs Chan told Granny that her family were going to the Chinese Dragon Festival and suggested that we meet up. Granny said we were looking forward to the event, and that sounded like a good idea.

I nodded in agreement. As far as I was concerned, as long as the festival wasn't on the following day when we were going to Rainbow End, I didn't mind.

Then, Mrs Chan poked around in her large floral handbag and produced a book. Handing it to me, she said, "Perhaps you'd like to read this legend. The story comes from the region where we live."

"Sorry, it's not about a nugget of gold," Mei Ling said with a little smile as she slipped a card in, "but it is about good fortune!"

I took the book and thanked them both. It was called 'The Dragon's Pearl'.

We parted company after I had exchanged numbers with Mei Ling, and we went off to Australia's oldest pottery, where they used to make sewers long ago. Nowadays, they make all sorts of pottery. We visited their museum first and then we watched the potters make lovely vases on the wheel. They let us take a go, and I found myself laughing at Granny's expression when her pot flopped down on one side. My pot wasn't any better, but she didn't laugh... Perhaps there was a glimmer of a smile, but she didn't laugh.

I suppose grannies can't help it if they don't believe in ghosts. Anyway, tomorrow we'd be off to Rainbow End after visiting the lawyer. Yippee!

CHAPTER 16
THE DRAGON'S PEARL

Back at the hotel, I pulled out The Dragon's Pearl from my bag, another gift from Mei Ling's family that would lead to further discoveries.

It was a paperback book full of striking pictures. On the front cover, a dragon, covered in fish scales with deer antlers and hawk talons extended, coiled snakelike around the frightened face of a young boy. I opened the book.

Long ago in the days of the cloud-breathing dragons, I read, *there lived a boy called Xiao Sheng. He was a happy lad and he loved to sing. Each day, he toiled from dawn to dusk cutting grass for sale in his local village. It was back-breaking work with little reward. Although his family were poor, Xiao was good-natured, and each day he would say to his mother as he was leaving, "Who knows what the gods have in store for us. Today may not be the same as yesterday."*

But every day turned out to be exactly the same, and at sunset he would return for his bowl of rice and a cup of tea before going to bed.

Then, one year, there was a terrible drought. Day after day, the sun beat down on the land. The river dried up and the crops failed. Even the grass shrivelled up and he had to travel further each day to cut grass for the market.

One day, as he was wearily climbing over the brow of a hill, he spied in the distance a field full of lush green grass. He rushed over and began to furiously cut the grass. He gathered a huge bunch and brought it to the village where it fetched a good price.

Each day, he returned to the same field and, lo and behold, each day the grass was fresh and ready for cutting again.

"Thank you, thank you!" he said, bowing to the gods. "Thank you for my good fortune."

Then, one day, he had a great idea. He decided that he would transplant the field of grass to a pasture close to his home.

He carefully cut away the sods with the pieces of grass and transported them home. All day, he laboured and, finally, when he was almost finished, he spotted something shimmering in the soil. He bent down and there, glowing in the dirt, was a beautiful, translucent pearl. Picking it up with great care, he carried the precious gem home to his mother.

"Look," he said. "See what the gods have given us."

His mother rejoiced at their good fortune and placed the precious pearl in the rice jar up on the ledge.

Next morning when Xiao awoke, he was very disappointed to discover that all the grass he had so carefully planted had completely withered.

"Oh, what have I done to upset the gods?" he asked. But his mother replied, "Look son, the gods have smiled on us. The jar is brimming with rice."

Xiao looked and he was amazed to see rice spilling on to the floor.

"It's a magic pearl," said his mother, full of joy. "Perhaps if we put it in the money jar, the same thing might happen."

They placed the pearl in the money jar and, in no time, the jar was full of golden coins.

"You are right," his happy mother said as she danced around the room. "Today is not the same as yesterday!"

No longer did Xiao toil in the hot sun. Instead, he visited his friends and neighbours, sharing the bounty that the pearl bestowed. The villagers were pleased that Xiao and his mother had found such happiness, and they were thankful for the kindness they received.

"How well the gods smile down on them," they said.

But there were two men who felt jealous of Xiao's good fortune and, one day, they burst into Xiao's hut and demanded money. They rummaged around in the room, breaking everything as they went and, eventually, they discovered the money jar.

"So here is the money," one of the men said, "but what is this?" he asked, as he picked out the beautiful, shimmering pearl from the centre of the jar.

"It's my magic pearl," said Xiao. "You can have the money, but the pearl is mine." And, with that, he snatched the pearl from the robber's hand and popped it into his mouth. The men grabbed him and yelled at him to spit it out. They shook him until his head nearly fell off, but he would not relinquish the pearl.

Fearing for the safety of her child, Xiao's mother beseeched him to spit out the pearl, but to no avail. Xiao's lips were firmly sealed around it. The robbers, enfuriated by his refusal to release the pearl, banged him against the wall. But, instead of spitting the pearl out, Xiao swallowed it with an enormous gulp.

Next minute, a burning heat filled his throat. He rushed to the water jar and emptied it. He rushed outside to the water barrel and emptied that. But his craving for water was not satisfied. He rushed to the riverbank and, kneeling down, he began to drink and drink.

"Stop! Stop!" his mother cried, but Xiao was unable to assuage the terrible thirst that had come upon him, and he could not stop.

He drank and drank and still the magic pearl burned within him. Great black clouds gathered in the sky, lightning split the heavens and the earth began to tremble, but still Xiao continued to drink.

His mother tried to drag him from the riverbank, but, even as she dragged, a great change began to come over the boy. Scales replaced skin as his body began to twist and wind like a snake, hands became talons and antlers sprouted from his head.

Petrified, she stared at the curling, swirling creature and, as he opened his mouth, his mother spied the gleaming pearl. Before her eyes, her son had transformed into a dragon.

Throwing back his mighty head, he absorbed cloud after cloud into his leathery lungs, and then, with a great thrust of his body, he expelled the clouds, and rain fell on the dry scorched earth.

The villagers screamed with delight and thanked the dragon for his benevolence. Now their crops would grow again and starvation would become but a distant memory.

Again and again, the dragon spewed rain on the thirsty earth until the puddles trickled into the streams and the streams flowed into the rivers, and the rivers swelled as they journeyed home to the sea.

It was a time of great rejoicing for the village folk. Apart from the fields owned by the two thieves, the rain fell everywhere and the crops began to grow in great profusion.

But for Xiao's mother it was a time of great sorrow. She knew her son had bestowed great wealth on the village but she felt her heart was breaking as she watched her one and only son swish his dragon tail against the bank for the last time, before disappearing into the depths of the swollen waters.

The village folk were kind to her and honoured the old woman and her son, and each day they brought grains of rice and tossed them into the river in thanksgiving for the gift of water to their valley.

The years have passed, but, even today, where the River Min flows through the province of Sichaun, the children still hear the story of The Dragon's Pearl from the old people in the village and, sometimes, if they listen very carefully to the rippling of the water, they can hear the sound of Xiao singing, "Today is not the same as yesterday".

I closed the book, imagining the dragon exploding the thunderstorm straight into my face and, as I lay back, my dragon joined all the other storybook dragons as they swooped through the skies and collided with Hans Christian Anderson characters. I wanted to join in their adventures. I wanted to fly high in the sky. I wanted to pretend.

I could feel my eyelids beginning to droop, and I was just beginning a fabulous dream when the book dropped with a plop on the ground and I remembered where I was.

How annoying.

I sat up grumpily and picked it up. Next thing, Mei Ling's card fell out. My goodness, I had forgotten about it. I began to read it out aloud to myself:

Dear Emily,

It is very pleasing for me to make an Irish friend. I hope your grandmother is fortunate and the mining company buys Rainbow End. I look forward to seeing you at the weekend for the festival.

Your friend,

Mei Ling

I looked again at the note. What a strange thing to write. Mei Ling had told me that her father was in charge of buying land for the mining company, but why would she think that the mining company wanted to buy Rainbow End? I thought it was her father who was interested in buying Rainbow End for his family. Maybe she just made a slip up when writing the note. It was strange though. I'd ask her about it at the festival.

CHAPTER 17
THE LAWYER

The next morning, we were sitting in the lawyer's office patiently waiting when the secretary entered and ushered us into Mr Bowman's room.

"Mr Bowman, your clients," she murmured. Mr Bowman rose from his chair. He was a tall man with wiry hair, and glasses that sat at the end of his nose. Behind the glasses were alert eyes and below his nose was a thin-lipped mouth.

"Mrs Clancy, I believe," he said. "Take a seat."

"Thank you," Gran replied. "I appreciate this meeting at such short notice." She motioned me forward. "This is my granddaughter, Emily McCleary."

He nodded at me. "Pleased to meet you," he said, waving me to a chair beside Gran with his spindly finger. Then he sat down again behind the mahogany table.

"How may I be of assistance to you?"

Gran leaned forward. "Recently, I inherited a property in this area."

"May I congratulate you on your good fortune," he said.

"I have inherited a property in Back Creek, Bendigo, and I wish to have it checked out with a view to making a sale."

"Back Creek," he said, his face sharpening as he peered over his spectacles.

"Yes," replied Gran. "I inherited it from my late father. He was a miner, you know."

"How interesting," murmured Mr Bowman, as he assessed Gran.

"He came out with my mother just after the war, and I believe he worked in the Central Deborah Mine for a number of years."

"A very important mine at the time," he said, his ferret eyes darting past me and over to Gran.

"Later," continued Gran, "he returned to Ireland, and retired there until his death twelve years ago."

"Twelve years ago," repeated Mr Bowman, listening intently. "And it is only now that you come looking for the property."

"Yes," said Gran. "His will only came to light quite recently."

"And I presume you have papers for the property?" Mr Bowman said tapping the table.

"Well, I have the will, if that is what you mean," Gran replied, as she poked around in her large leather handbag and produced the envelope. He took the proffered envelope, opened it, picked out the will and began to read. And as he read, he became very still.

"Rainbow End," he muttered to himself, as his sharp, beady eyes scanned the will. When he had finished, there was silence as he adjusted his spectacles. Then he spoke in a thin, reedy voice. "Of course, you have a Certificate of Title for this property?"

"I'm afraid I don't know exactly what a Certificate of Title is," replied Gran, looking a bit foolish.

Mr Bowman raised an eyebrow. "It's an official record of ownership, Mrs Clancy."

"Oh," said Gran. "I wonder..."

"Not to worry," Mr Bowman interrupted, "That's a minor detail and we'll be able to conduct a title search for you."

After studying the will for another few moments, he cleared his throat and enquired, "And do you have a map of the property?"

"No. Perhaps there's one with the certificate," Gran replied.

"We'll look into it," he said, his eyes twitching nervously.

He looked at the will again and I could see something was ticking over in his brain.

"I wonder could you give me some details about the property?" he asked, taking out his pen.

"Rainbow End," she replied, "belonged to my father, but he left the place over fifty years ago. There was a recession and nobody was interested in buying land. It's gone to complete rack and ruin. Perhaps you are familiar with it?"

His slit eyes twitched slightly again as he shifted in his chair.

"I am familiar with the general area, but not with the specific property," he said. "You mentioned that it is your intention to sell the property."

"Well, as soon as possible," said Gran, "I'm over here in Australia for just a short time, and I should like to have as many loose ends tied up as is practicable."

"Well, I'll need to change the title details into your name before it can be put on the market."

"Do you think it would be a saleable property?" asked Gran.

The lawyer hesitated momentarily. "I think there are distinct possibilities. Has it been valued?" he enquired.

"Not yet," said Gran.

"In that case, perhaps I could recommend a real estate agent to you."

"That would be very kind of you," Gran said.

"Mr Kent is his name. I'll get in contact with him straight away. He might be able to fit you in for an appointment in the near future."

Bowman dialled a number on his mobile. "Please excuse me," he said rising up. "I'll be back in a moment," and he left the room to make the call.

After waiting for ages, I needed to go to the toilet, so I followed the signs down a long corridor and up the stairs to the right. I was quietly going about my business when I overheard Mr Bowman in his upstairs office. "No, she has no idea about the value of the property."

I craned to hear, but I heard no more as he closed the door.

Shortly afterwards, he returned smiling broadly. "Mr Kent has a cancellation, and I'm pleased to say that he will be able to fit you in for an appointment tomorrow."

"That's terrific," said Granny.

"Would 1.30pm be suitable?" asked Mr Bowman.

"Perfect," said Gran.

"So shall I confirm the appointment?"

"Please," said Granny.

"Now, I must warn you that it will take some time to check out the authenticity of the property with the Victorian Land Register, but I'll fast-forward the process if I can," said Mr Bowman solemnly.

"Thank you," said Gran. "I would appreciate it."

"Once we have established the ownership of the property, we will be in a position to put it on the market," Mr Bowman said, extending his hand towards Gran. "I'm sure we'll be able to find a suitable client."

We rose to leave and, as we left the office, Gran whispered to me.

"Wouldn't it be amazing if we could sell the property before we go home?"

"I suppose so," I said, feeling that something about Mr Bowman didn't seem quite right, and I wondered should I mention to Granny what I had heard upstairs, but she was so excited, I just decided to keep my mouth shut. That was a foolish decision, but I didn't know it at the time.

CHAPTER 18
THE ESTATE AGENT

Next day, we had a quick fish and chips for lunch and were in Mr Kent's office at 1.25pm. On the dot of 1.30pm Mr Kent arrived.

"G'day ladies," he said, sweeping a large, leather hat off his head. "You must be Mrs Clancy."

He gave Granny a big handshake. "And this must be your daughter," he said throwing a glance in my direction.

"Actually, Mr Kent, she's my granddaughter," said Granny, smiling and clearly feeling twenty years younger.

"Call me Jake," he said, eyeing Granny up. "We don't stand on ceremony in this part of the world."

"Pleased to hear it," said Gran. "I'm May and this is Emily."

"Ah, the baby of the family," he said, patting me on the head.

That did it. I couldn't stand the man; arrogant creep. I glared at him.

"No," I said. "This isn't the baby. Babies are a different size."

"Touché, touché," he said, winking at Granny.

"I'm not Touché," I said, "I'm Emily McCleary."

"No offence, no offence," he said, smoothly, and then he totally ignored me and lavished all his attention on Granny, who was thoroughly enjoying it. He admired her youthful looks and praised her for travelling all the way from Ireland on such a long and difficult journey. Granny lapped it all up and described her surprise and delight when she discovered that she had inherited Rainbow End.

She explained that there were approximately twenty acres involved, and he told her that he had a client who was looking for that exact acreage close to the town and that his client would be delighted to rebuild the homestead and restore it to its former glory.

"You'll have no trouble selling that. Properties are fetching good prices in that area."

"Are you sure?" asked Gran. "What sort of valuation would you put on it?"

"Well, I'd have to see it first, but twenty acres with a house would fetch good money."

I knew people looked for lifestyle plots, but I wondered what type of person would wish to buy such a scabby piece of land with such a tumble-down house, but I said nothing.

Then I thought of Mei Ling's dad, and thought somebody like him might build a new house there.

"I'm delighted to hear such good news," said Gran, "but are you familiar with the actual property?"

"No, but should you care to show me its exact location, I'll get on the job immediately, and in no time you'll be returning to Ireland with your daughter, a wealthy woman."

I said nothing, just curled my lip.

"And when would it be a good time for you to go and see the property?" asked my Gran, perkily.

"Straight away, if you'd like," he said, with a charming smile. "A client called off today, so I've a free afternoon."

"Our good fortune," said Granny, turning to me. "Emily, I think we have met a most competent young man." I bit my lip, but said nothing.

We left shortly after, Mr Kent – or should I say Jake – leading the way in his green Ute, with us following in the white Toyota.

When we reached Rainbow End, Jake turned into Granny's hero when he valued the property, and she couldn't credit the enormous sum of money he mentioned.

"It's incredible," she said. "I never thought it would be worth so much. Are you sure about this?"

"Absolutely," he replied. "I'll have no trouble getting that sum for you."

"My goodness," said Gran in amazement.

"So you'll sell at that price?"

"Well, I'll certainly consider it," Gran replied. And I knew by her tone of voice that she would snap up the price the minute she was offered it.

"I understand that Bowman is having the deeds checked out," said the wonderful Jake, "and when that's sorted out, I'll be in contact with my client. If he is prepared to purchase, I'll be back to you and we'll sort out a deal."

He smiled again. "How's that for efficiency?" he added, leering at me. I turned my back on the toad and looked elsewhere.

"Sounds good to me," said Gran, smiling broadly.

"Well, I'd better be off now," Jake said, sitting into his car. "Good doing business with you... and your daughter," and away he zoomed in a cloud of dust.

Some people just have a very bad effect on me...Yuck.

CHAPTER 19
FINDING THE MAP

Granny was in a great mood, so the minute Mr Kent left, I directed her straight over to the sideboard. It was a funny piece of furniture. Obviously, it had been built with a lot of care because the wood was smooth and straight, but now it just looked neglected. I pulled out the drawers that Granny had so carefully pushed in. Of course, there was nothing inside them except rubbish. Everything of any value had disappeared.

But then I noticed that the back of the sideboard was made of a different colour wood, so I started tapping at the back, hoping that something would miraculously move and out would pop my nugget of gold. But, unfortunately, nothing happened.

"I don't think we're in luck," I said, wrinkling up my face.

"Maybe, you're looking in the wrong place," Gran said as she examined the drawers minutely. Suddenly, I saw what she meant. Old sheets of The Bendigo Advertiser lined the drawers. I grabbed a drawer, emptied the contents, and began to tear off the lining and scratch on the wood.

"For goodness' sake, will you stop," said Gran. "Don't you know that a false bottom is always underneath the first layer of wood? Come here and I'll show you."

I brought over the empty drawer and Granny began to tap around the edges.

"Nothing here," she said. "We'll try another one." So I handed her the second one, which had a little red ribbon in the corner.

"Do you know what that ribbon represents?" she asked, holding up the little reddish-brown rag.

"No," I said impatiently.

"Well that, my dear, was probably used by the miner who lived here during the Red Ribbon revolution. The miners who refused to pay the miner's licence wore the ribbon as a sort of badge."

I handed her the third drawer. "What about this one?"

She took the drawer, turned it upside down and, after pouring out the stuff, she looked at the lining.

"You know," she said, "there's an article on the Red Ribbon Revolution here on the newspaper lining."

"Oh," I said, knowing that Granny wouldn't proceed to find the false bottom until the article had been read. "What does it say?"

"It says," she said, not looking at the newspaper at all, "that the miners were successful." And she continued to tap around the third drawer. Suddenly, she stopped and her eyes lit up. I could feel the adrenaline pump around my body.

"I think you were right, Emily. I think we're in business," she said, as she tapped the base of the wood. "There's something here." And with that, out slid the false floor followed by a piece of parchment, which landed plop on the floor.

"Oh Granny, I wonder what it is?" I said, picking up the paper. My hands were shaking and my heart was beating at a ferocious speed.

"Perhaps, you'd better give it to me," said Gran, as she took the parchment from me and rolled it out carefully.

"It looks like an old map of the place."

"Granny, perhaps it shows where Pa put the nugget."

"You might be right, but the light is gone again and I can't see," said Granny, peering at the old fashioned handwriting.

I tried to read the map myself, but the ink had faded and it was difficult to see its outlines.

"Come on," said Gran. "We'll be able to see it more clearly in the light at the hotel."

I clutched the map to my chest. "Okay," I said, heading for the car straight away.

Eventually, we reached the hotel, and I was just speeding up the stairs when I bumped into the lady at the counter.

"Hello," she said, with a big smile. "And did you find that nugget of gold yet?"

I stopped, "No, but we're going treasure hunting tomorrow."

"Sounds exciting. Can I come too?" she said, jokingly.

"Sure," I said, "Just as long as you remember who owns the nugget."

She laughed.

"You'd be very welcome," said Gran, smiling.

"Are you sure?" she said, in a surprised voice.

"Absolutely," said Gran.

"Well, maybe I'll take you up on that one. Thanks."

"See you tomorrow," I said, scrambling past her up the stairs. I couldn't wait to examine the old map in my hand. "Granny will tell you when we're going."

Up in our bedroom, I sat at the reading desk and turned on the light. At the back of the sheet were the names

Tom Bryan 1859-1901
Phil Hannigan 1901-1945
Patrick O'Neill 1945

Printed in the corner were the words Carruthers and Sons Ltd.

I turned the sheet over. It was an old, handwritten map. On the top right-hand corner was the title, *Sketch Map of Rainbow End, 1859*.

It showed Back Creek with the iron bark gum trees growing up the banks and, along the creek, there was an area called 'alluvial workings'. The tracks were marked with a dark dotted line, and the house was marked with a little circle beside the trees. I examined it in great detail and, when she came in, I showed Granny the map.

"What are those light-coloured dots down at the bottom?" I asked.

She put on her reading glasses and peered at the map.

"I'm not sure," she said, "but I imagine that's the southern boundary of the homestead. The tracks at the top are the roads, and they form the boundary to the north and east of the place." She looked up, "Any sign of the nugget on the map?"

"Nothing definite," I said, taking the map again and studying it hard. It was then that I noticed a tiny mark where the road touched the southern boundary line. "What do you think of that mark?" I asked her. "It's in pencil, isn't it?"

"You're right, I think, but my eyes aren't great," she replied.

"And if it's in pencil, it probably was put in much later on."

"Probably," said Gran, "but don't get your hopes up. Tomorrow is another day and it's bedtime now, so good night and sleep tight."

CHAPTER 20
DREAMTIME

I thought I wouldn't sleep, but I did. In fact, I slept so well that Granny had to wake me in the morning. After breakfast, we went downtown, rented a metal detector and picked up the hotel lady before heading away.

"By the way," she said, jumping into the front seat beside Gran, "I never introduced myself. I'm Alkira, but everyone calls me Kira for short. It means 'the sky'."

Kira turned out to be a very chatty person with a great interest in everybody and, as Granny chatted to her, we discovered that her grandmother had been an Aborigine.

"That's why I'm so dark-skinned," she explained, and she began to tell us about the Kulin people, which is an umbrella name for a group of six nations.

"The group I'm from is called the Djadjawurung people," she said, "You pronounce that Jarjarwrung. But most folk simply call us the Jaara folk."

Well, that makes it simpler to remember, I thought.

She pulled out a map of Bendigo and showed us a place just north of the town. "That's Eaglehawk, and the eaglehawk is our moiety."

I'd never heard the word moiety, so I asked her what it meant.

"It's like our special family emblem, I guess," she replied. "In this area, some Aborigines have the eaglehawk as their moiety and others have the raven."

She turned to me solemnly. "You know," she said, "you're very lucky that I'm coming along today, because the eaglehawk is a symbol of good fortune. In our culture, the eaglehawk overcomes adversity."

"So you think we'll find the nugget of gold today," I quipped.

"Well, the eaglehawk always succeeds in the face of difficulty."

I didn't know if she was joking or not, so I nodded in agreement and then asked about the raven moiety.

"Not quite so lucky," she replied. "You know my great-gran used to tell me a story about the eaglehawk and the ravencrow. Would you like to hear it?"

"Sure," I said, hoping she'd finish the story before we reached Rainbow End.

She took a deep breath and began to speak.

"Long, long ago, there was an eaglehawk called Wildu. He was a magnificent creature and, as king of the birds, he spent his time bossing around his nephews, the Wakarla crows, and telling them what they could eat or couldn't eat."

She screwed herself around so she could see me in the backseat. "You know what colour a crow is?"

"Black," I replied.

"Well, at the beginning of this story the crows are white, and," she said, facing out the window again, "these white crows hated their uncle, so one day they decided to get rid of him."

She waved her hands vaguely to the right. "They flew up to Ulkananha, which is north west of here, and made a fake stick-rat's nest. They got some kangaroo leg bones, sharpened them up and stuck them into the nest with the sharp bits sticking up. Then they persuaded Wildu to come and stamp on the nest. He never saw the bones, and the sharp bits went right up through his feet before entering his body."

Pointing into the distance at a low-lying mound, she continued. "Somehow, he managed to drag himself from the nest and, although he was bleeding and dying, he flew to a hill overlooking Ipaathantha, where a great ceremony at the boro ground was being held. However, when the creatures saw him, instead of helping him, they laughed at him."

Kira leaned over the seat to me again. "It was cruel," she said, "especially as Wildu was such a proud creature. But," she said, straightening up, "despite his injuries, he rose up into the air and flew north to Yurdlawarta where he died, and the story goes that his feathers turned to flint."

Her eyes fixed on the imaginary scene, and she whispered, "But that wasn't the end of it."

She paused. "When his wives left the ceremony and discovered their dead husband with his feathers scattered around him, they were upset and kept breathing into him... and guess what happened?"

"What?"

"As they breathed into him, he began to move again and come back from the dead. And the next minute," she said in a scary voice, "he was up in the air, and he was so mad that he was threatening to eat all the creatures who had been mocking him."

She turned and looked directly into my eyes. "And, as he flew away, he ordered his wives to dig a tunnel into a cave and to lead all the creatures down the tunnel while he raised a storm to punish his nephews. Then he told his wives to sleep at the entrance of the tunnel." Her voice quavered. "And that night," she continued, "he raised a great storm and all the creatures fled down the tunnel for safety. But the cave was not as safe a place as they had imagined because, as soon as they were all down, Wildu built a huge fire in the entrance, which spread down the tunnel into the cave." She paused for effect. "The wives, the animals and the white cockatoos near the entrance escaped but the rest of the birds were trapped. Somehow the magpies and the willy wagtails escaped with only getting a little burnt, but the crows were burnt to black crisp."

Then she stopped and gazed at me, and I found myself muttering, "And that explains why they're black now?"

"That's the reason," she replied. "And that's why you're glad my moiety is an eaglehawk and not a raven."

There was silence, then Gran spoke. "That was a fairly grim story."

"Most Aboriginal stories are," said Kira with a laugh. "They're our version of the creation stories. Rather gruesome, like some of the Bible stories."

"Very true," agreed Gran swinging the car into her parking spot beside the bridge, "but now it's treasure time. Where's that map?"

CHAPTER 21
THE TREASURE HUNT

As soon as the car came to a halt, I handed the wizened map to Gran for examination.

"Can you see the mark?" I asked, dying to get going.

"Yes," she said, looking intently at the map. "It seems to me that we must walk along the northern boundary until we reach the place where it touches the western boundary."

"Time to go," I said jumping out of the car.

"Nugget time," agreed Gran, closing the map. "Emily, you can carry the shovel, I'll bring the map and Kira can bring the detector since she knows how to operate the gadget."

I started out at a great pace, but I soon discovered that the detector operator wasn't going to be rushed. She was an Aborigine, she told us, and Aborigines take their time.

So as we walked slowly up the hill, Kira would stop frequently to point out something to us.

Granny was very patient, but I thought I'd go mad. This slow pace of life didn't suit me at all when there was treasure to be found.

However, Kira was full of stories and she wasn't going anywhere in a hurry, so I had to contain myself. It wasn't easy.

Kira said the stories came from her Aboriginal great-grandmother, who had lived out in the bush.

When she saw the little stream, she told us that the Aborigines never caught the first kangaroo that came to a water hole. They allowed all the kangaroos to come and go, and they always waited to trap the last kangaroo. This meant that the first kangaroos were not frightened of the water hole, so they could be caught another day.

She showed us different plants that the women used to pick to make a sticky paste for eating. She also showed us how the Aborigines cut out plates from the bark of gum trees.

Her knowledge was incredible, but all I could think about was my nugget of gold.

Eventually, after many delays, we reached the summit. Beads of excitement broke out on my forehead. Even the other two were getting a bit excited. We walked along the northern boundary and, believe it or not, we found a large mound of stones under the trees, exactly where the pencil mark was on the map.

"This must be the place," I said, pointing to the heap. "I'm sure it is. It was obviously specially built to mark the spot."

"Perhaps," said Kira in her easy, non-committal way as she started up the detector, "but maybe it's only a grave for a pet."

I watched anxiously as the detector slowly moved across the stones. Then, all of a sudden, the detector started clicking. It made a real clickety-clackety sound.

"I think we should dig here," said Kira, taking the shovel from me.

She started to dig. She dug and dug and dug. I could feel my heart bursting with excitement. The shovel was scratching off something and it didn't look like earth. I shut my eyes. I just couldn't watch.

"Sorry," said Kira, "just a bean can and some old bones."

She started walking around with the detector again, moving it slowly from side to side. Nothing happened for a long time. Then it started to click very loudly. It became more and more insistent.

"The shovel again, please," Kira said, digging into the dry, arid soil. "Maybe we'll be lucky this time." She dug and dug again, but this time she unearthed an old frying pan. The next time it was an old coin. After that, a paint can and then a couple of bottle tops.

Finally, I could contain myself no longer. "I think it's my turn now," I said, grabbing the detector. "Maybe I'll be lucky. Maybe the nugget wants me to find it."

I frantically swished the detector under an outcrop of rocks and, suddenly, the detector went absolutely wild. "I have it! I have it," I screamed, starting to dance around.

"Hold your horses," said Kira beginning to scrape underneath the rock. She scratched and scratched using a nail like implement she produced from her pocket.

"There's something here, alright," she said, and I could see Gran's eyes beginning to shine as Kira picked away for another couple of minutes.

"I can see it! I can see it," I screamed.

"It's there in the corner," said Gran pointing up to the right.

Kira put in her finger and, after another bit of scraping, she tickled a large, shiny lump out from the right hand corner.

"Oh," said Gran, holding her breath. "It's the luck of the Irish."

"Hmmm," said Kira spitting on the lump and holding it to the light. "Unfortunately, all that glitters is not gold."

"What do you mean?" I asked.

"I'm afraid," said Kira, "it's only a lump of pyrite."

"But it looks like gold," I blurted out.

"Just fake gold," replied Kira. "Shiny, but worthless."

"What a shame," said Gran, taking the lump and rolling the pyrite around in her hand. "So disappointing."

We went fossicking again, but found absolutely nothing else. Finally, Kira stopped altogether.

"I don't think we're very successful," she said, sitting down heavily on a rock. "Perhaps I might take another look at that map?"

Gran pulled out the map and presented it to her. She looked at the names on the outside.

"So these are the folk who owned Rainbow End since 1859."

"Yes," I said, beginning to tell her about finding the map in the sideboard. "These are the people who owned Rainbow End and there's Pa's name at the bottom. He bought the land from Phil Hannigan."

"That's most interesting," she said, looking keenly at us. "And who do you think owned the land before all these people?"

"The government," I answered up, smartly. "They sold the land to Tom Bryan in 1859."

"And who do you think owned it before the government?" she asked.

I was stumped. "I suppose it was the Jaara people," I replied.

"I suppose so," she replied raising an eyebrow. "I wonder if they got a good price for it?" and she said no more.

After a moment, she leaned back in pensive mode.

"You know," she said, changing the subject as she looked at me, "my dad used to be always joking with our Pa about his nugget of gold. Dad would ask him where he'd hidden the old lump, and your Pa would say, 'And where do you think himself would hide his crock?'"

"That was a strange thing to say," I said. "Who was 'himself' and what is a crock?"

"Well a crock of gold was a pot of gold, but I'm not sure about the 'himself' bit. All I know is that it was a standing joke between them," said Kira, "and your Pa always said the same thing."

"But who was 'himself'?" I enquired again, turning this time towards Gran.

She pondered for a moment, and then she replied with a twinkle. "I'm guessing 'himself' was a leprechaun, because leprechauns are the only people I've ever known to have a crock of gold"

"So was it a type of riddle?" I asked.

"Perhaps," she replied.

"And Pa's riddle had something to do with the leprechauns in Ireland long ago."

"Perhaps."

"And…" I said, willing her to continue. She smiled again, winked at Kira and obligingly elaborated on her explanation.

"The fairy folk had shoemakers for mending their shoes, and these fairy shoemakers were called leprechauns, and..."

"And these leprechauns always had a crock of gold," added Kira, "according to the old yarns."

"What old yarns?" I asked, mystified.

"Well," said Gran, settling herself on the bank, "according to the old yarns, leprechauns were wealthy folk because the fairies were constantly dancing the nights away, and their dainty shoes were constantly in need of repair."

"And what had that to do with a crock?" I asked.

"Oh," she said, "the crock was where the leprechauns kept their fairy money, and that..." She paused. "... was hidden at the end of the rainbow."

All of a sudden, a bell went off in my brain. "That's it, Granny," I said. "That's the answer."

"What's the answer?" she asked.

"The nugget," I said, getting excited. "The nugget is in the house. It's up inside Rainbow End. Come on."

I started running up to the ramshackle house, dragging poor Granny with me.

"It's in the house. It must be in the house," I shouted. "Come on!"

We reached the house and started pulling things out. We checked the sideboard again. We looked under cupboards, behind cupboards, on top of cupboards. We looked under floorboards, in jam jars, under the threshold stone, in the curtain seams. Everywhere you could possibly imagine. We searched for a whole hour and we found nothing. Absolutely nothing. Finally, there was nowhere else to search.

"It's already gone," I whispered, my voice disappearing into a whimper.

"I think you're right," said Gran propping herself up on the old bed.

"That's why the house was in such a mess when we first came," I said. "Somebody came and stole the nugget."

Gran nodded in silent agreement.

I kicked the leg of the chair. "So Lady Deborah just didn't get it right this time."

"Well, you never know. Prayers aren't always answered immediately," Granny said, patting me on the shoulder.

"And the eaglehawk didn't bring any luck either," I said, scowling across at Kira.

"Time will tell," said Kira. "But, in the meantime, since we have difficulties discovering the Australian nugget of gold, let's go home to my place and discover a bit more about the Irish crocks of gold from that old grandfather of mine."

CHAPTER 22
THE DISAPPOINTMENT

I sat in the back of the car. You know, that thing called disappointment is very hard to swallow. I tried to listen to Granny chatting to Kira, but I just couldn't concentrate. All I could think about was the nugget of gold.

Every now and then, a big noisy gulp would escape out of me, and then it would get caught going down my throat. Granny was very sympathetic, but what could she say? All the sympathy in the world wouldn't find me my nugget of gold. Gone were my dreams of paying back all the debts.

When everything felt just horrible, Gran's phone rang and I discovered that things could get even more horrible. She pulled over to the side of the road and put it to her ear.

"Oh, good afternoon, Mr Bowman."

I pricked up when I saw Gran take a sharp intake of breath.

"You're very sorry about what?" Gran frowned. "You are unable to locate the certificate of title for the property."

She moved the phone to the other ear. "What exactly do you mean? Has it been mislaid?" She rubbed her forehead. "Perhaps it has been filed in a different location. You say Melbourne is where the land register is held." She ran her fingers through her hair. "Surely there must be some document that shows the transaction."

Mr Bowman mumbled something on the phone, which I couldn't hear. There was silence and then Gran said, "This seems very strange to me. I have travelled halfway across the world with a will which says that Patrick O'Neill owned the property, and now you're telling me that the will is invalid."

I could hear Bowman muttering something else in the background, and then there was another shocked silence before Gran spoke again. "Are you telling me that there is absolutely no record of Pa owning Rainbow End?"

Bowman muttered something again, but, though I listened intently, I couldn't figure out what he was saying.

"But," Gran stuttered, "we found a map on the property with Patrick O'Neill's name on it, so he must have owned it."

There was a brief silence on the other end of the phone. Then Bowman mumbled something I again couldn't hear before Gran replied. "So you're telling me that Pa might have lived on Rainbow End, but he never actually owned it? This seems very odd."

Gran paused as she considered the information she was receiving. "But if he lived there, shouldn't he have squatters' right after a certain length of time?"

There was more muttering from the other end of the phone.

"I know he left Rainbow End fifty years ago, but he must have some rights."

How I wished I could hear Bowman's responses. I peeled my ears.

"This is unbelievable," said Gran, acidly. "My father would hardly have bequeathed something to me if he didn't own it. There must be a mistake. What exactly is the protocol for checking out a situation like this?"

I heard Bowman speaking again and Gran responded, "Okay, I'll do that. You say that I can go online and for a small fee I can check out the details on the Torrens Land Register System in Melbourne. I'm sure this matter can be sorted out. Good day, Mr Bowman."

She switched off the phone and stared ahead. Finally, she spoke. "Apparently, the will is invalid because there is no certificate of title, so legally Pa never owned Rainbow End. Mr Bowman seems to think that Pa just thought he owned it."

I put my arms around Granny and I promised to look up the situation online but that didn't seem to help. Granny was just devastated.

Eventually, she turned on the car engine and turned to Kira. "Sounds like there is no pot of gold at the end of the Rainbow for me either."

"Don't be too sure about that," replied Kira. "Property rights in Australia are a bit strange sometimes."

CHAPTER 23
THE IRISH CROCK

Eventually, we reached the house where Kira's grandpa lived. As we got out of the car, I slipped my hand into Gran's. Her dreams were ended, too. I could feel her terrible disappointment, and yet something inside me wondered if the old man might have the answer to the riddle about the nugget of gold. I couldn't help myself from perking up a bit.

His house was lovely and old-fashioned, with a tin roof and a veranda out the front. Kira brought us into the living room and there in the corner was a very old man in an armchair.

"Hello, Grandpa," said Kira, rubbing his shoulder. "I've brought some visitors to see you."

The doddering old man turned his head towards us. "Matt Henson the fiddler, ladies," he said, as he extended a very shaky hand. "How can I be of service?"

"This is Mrs Clancy and her granddaughter Emily, from Ireland."

"Pleased to meet you," he said.

"And," added Kira, mischievously, "these Irish folk are very special people."

"Why so?" he asked.

"Because," Kira said, "Mrs Clancy's father was called Patrick O'Neill."

The old man's eyes opened wide. "Not Pa O'Neill from the town of Cork?"

"The very same man," said Kira.

"Well, you are very welcome indeed," said Matt. "Come in and sit down. Tell me," he asked leaning forward, "how is Pa?"

There was a moment's hesitation, then Gran replied. "Long dead, I'm afraid."

Matt leaned back again and nodded. "Time marches on," he muttered to himself, and you could see his mind rambling back through the years. "Time marches on."

There was a yawning silence, broken by the ticking of the clock on the wall. Then Gran smiled at the old man and asked, "And how are you?"

And that little question opened a floodgate of conversation. You'd think nobody had spoken to him for a month. There was no stopping him. The little old man just came to life and started chatting away, and we just listened.

He told one yarn after another. Granny called him an old seanchaí and he was delighted. He spun stories about the miners down Central Deborah Mine, and, despite our treasure disappointments, we couldn't stop laughing.

"And when are you going down the mine?" he enquired.

"We've just been," said Gran

"Well, and did you meet the Lady Deborah?" he asked.

"Not me personally, but Emily did," she said, winking at him.

"You may laugh," he said seriously, "but it's a long time since there was a sighting and, whenever the Lady appears, there's gold in her wake."

There was silence, then Gran spoke. "Oh," she said, changing the subject, "that reminds me. I have a favour to ask you. Will you tell my granddaughter, Emily, the story about the leprechaun and the crock of gold?"

"No bother at all to me," he replied. "Just wait until I put on my seanchaí hat."

As he fumbled around for his hat, Kira whispered to us, "You mustn't interrupt him."

"Okay," I whispered back, and Kira winked.

Then the old man put the ancient, felt hat on his head and he began to tell his story in a strange voice. His accent was really funny, but I said nothing.

"Once upon a time," he began, "when the little people still roamed the countryside of Ireland, a young farmer's boy by the name of Jack was travelling home across the mountain one day when he heard a tip-tapping coming from the bushes. Being a curious fellow, he sneaked up to take a look. And what did he see, but a little man with a green jacket and a pointed cap, and sticking into the cap was a white owl's feather. The man was sitting cross-legged on a rock and he was mending a tiny shoe that shone like pure gold.

"Jack could hardly contain his excitement. In front of him was a leprechaun and Jack knew that every leprechaun had a crock of gold, and Jack was consumed by a greedy desire to possess this particular little man's crock. He also knew that, if his gaze left the leprechaun for an instant, the little man would disappear into thin air. He took a step forward.

"'Bail ó Dhia ar an obair,' said Jack, fixing his eyes on the little man. 'You're very busy this day.'

"'I am indeed,' said the leprechaun, springing up in surprise. 'I'd be kept busy making fairy shoes for fairy folk.'

"He tapped away for a bit and then he picked up his bottle off the ground. 'I don't suppose you'd like a sup?' he said, offering the bottle to Jack.

"Now Jack was just about to take the bottle when he suddenly remembered that he must keep his eye firmly fixed on the little man. 'It isn't interested in your bottle I am, but in your crock of gold.' And with that, he bent down and grabbed the leprechaun by the collar. He dangled him up in the air and shook him like a rag.

"'Now tell me,' Jack demanded in a loud voice, 'where it is that you've hidden that crock of gold.'

"'No need to get violent,' said the leprechaun, shaking visibly in his little black boots with the shiny buckles. 'Where else would you find a crock of gold but at the end of the rainbow?'

"'And where would that be?' asked Jack.

"'Just behind you,' answered the leprechaun, pointing to a spot behind Jack. In the nick of time, Jack remembered not to let the fairy man out of his sight. He squeezed him harder.

"'No more tricks, Mr Leprechaun. Show me where you keep your crock of gold this very minute or I'll beat the life out of you.' The little man screamed in fear as Jack began to squeeze his bones.

"'There's no need to hurt me. The crock you're looking for is hiding under the very stone you're standing on.'

"'Then swear to me on your honour that you're telling the truth and I'll let you go.'

"'I swear on my honour, and on the honour of the Munster fairies,' he said, 'that my crock is under the stone.'

"'Alright so,' said Jack, releasing him. 'Away with you.'

"Slán, is go n-eirí an t-ádh leat,"said the leprechaun, with a glint in his eye, before he vanished into thin air.

"With that, Jack headed home to get his spade as fast as his legs could carry him. But, alas for Jack, when he returned with his spade, he discovered that the whole mountain was covered in stones, and he couldn't remember under which stone the infamous crock of gold had been hidden. He was furious. The leprechaun had tricked him and, though he dug a hole under a thousand stones, he never found that crock of gold."

CHAPTER 24
JOHNNY MAC

There was a deep silence. Then Gran began to clap as Matt took off the storyteller's hat.

"Did I tell it right?" he enquired.

"You did a great job," Gran replied. "A story like that needs the skills of a seanchaí."

"So, do you know anything about a nugget of gold found at Rainbow End?" I said, suddenly remembering why I had wanted to visit the old man.

"Pa's nugget?"

"Yes," I replied. "The nugget of gold he found under the roots."

"Ah," said Matt, "Pa was a wily old boy. Any time I ever questioned him on its whereabouts, he'd always answer, with a smile, 'Where do you think himself would hide his crock?'"

"I know that," I said, "but what did it mean?"

"I'm afraid, child, I never found the answer to that one. But there was a different nugget of gold found in Pa's stick, and I do know about that nugget."

Suddenly, I felt Gran stiffen. "You mean the nugget he stole from the mine?" she asked.

"The very nugget, but your Pa didn't steal it."

"What do you mean?" Gran asked, edging closer to the old man.

"It's a long story," he said, taking a deep breath as he patted the seat beside him. "Sit down here my girl and I'll tell you all about it."

He closed his eyes as his mind drifted into the past. Then he looked directly at Gran. "I'm glad to meet the daughter of my best friend, Pa O'Neill. He was a great man and he was wronged."

Granny said nothing, just listened.

"It was that auld scoundrel Johnny Mac. He was always on the bottle and he never had a bob. One day, I thought he must have found a bit of a nugget down the mine, because he was full of glee, but he never said a word to anyone. The days went past, and I thought I was just imagining it, but it wasn't so long after that a nugget was found in Pa's stick."

"But how did that happen?" I asked.

"Well," Matt said, turning to me, "each morning, Pa used to bring his walking stick down the mine and, each evening, he'd bring it back up again. It must have come to Johnny that if he could borrow Pa's stick for an afternoon, he could make a little hole at the top of the stick and cover it with a screw-down lid, and, unbeknownst to Pa, he could place his little nugget in the secret space and Pa would bring it up for him."

"But why didn't he just hide the nugget in his clothes?" I asked.

"When they came up from the mine," Kira whispered at me, "the miners always had to take off their clothes for inspection while they had a shower, and the caretaker, Pop Spooner, would check the clothes if see if anyone had stolen gold from the mine."

"The nugget wasn't very big," continued Matt, "but it was big enough to buy his fare back to Ireland. The man was very homesick, and I suppose he badly wanted to go home, to see the green land and the people he loved."

"And my Pa got caught," said Gran, creasing her forehead.

"Yes," said Matt slowly. "Your Pa got caught for a crime he didn't commit, it was reported to Mr Rowe, and there was nothing any of us could do about it. The stolen nugget was found in his stick."

"And he went to jail," said Gran. "For something he didn't do."

The silence hung heavily.

"I suppose Johnny never thought the ragpicker would check the stick," Matt said.

I could feel Granny taking a deep breath. "Did nobody speak up for my Pa?"

"Of course we did," replied the old boy indignantly, "but it was no good. We all knew that Johnny had stolen the nugget, but we'd no proof."

"So Pa went to jail for two whole years. That wicked man let an innocent man take the blame," said Gran, her words creeping slowly out.

"It was a terrible thing to happen to the poor man," said Matt, looking again at Granny. "And when he was inside, your mam took you home to Ireland. And then he heard you'd died. It nearly broke his heart and, when he came out, no one would give him a job and he just hit the bottle."

"Pa wrote me a letter, you know," Gran said in a deadpan voice, "telling me just that."

"Communication was bad in those days," said old Matt, his voice quavering with age as he looked sympathetically at Gran. "A lad from home brought a letter with the news, but he lost the letter and he told Pa that your mother and yourself had died."

"No wonder the Aunts had no time for him," said Gran. "No wonder they called him a jailbird and a drunk."

"It was just poor communication," said Matt.

"You know that man's cowardice deprived me of my dad," said Gran, her eyes full of pain. "He deprived me of my childhood." She whispered quietly to herself, "I never knew the truth."

Then she turned to the old man. "All my life, I felt abandoned by my father. I hated him for stealing, I hated him for going to jail, I hated him for being an alcoholic, but most of all I hated him for not being around when I was growing up... and now I know that all that hatred was a waste."

"I'm sorry," replied Matt. "Your father was the best friend I ever had."

"And did Johnny ever confess to the crime?" I asked.

"Well, strangely enough, years later, he did confess. One night, when he was drunk as a skunk, he broke down and told everybody what he'd done."

"And was he thrown in jail?" I asked.

"That poor man met a much worse fate," Matt replied, "but that was no good to your dad."

"Didn't Pa ever know?" I inquired.

"No. I lost contact with him when he went back to Ireland, so he never knew."

I looked at Gran. She was sitting motionless. Finally, she spoke. "You know," she said, stumbling over her words, "I feel like a weight has been lifted off me. Now I can put the past to rest. I know that Pa loved me. He was an honest, good, caring man, and that means the world to me."

"And," said Kira, nudging us back into the present, "I think that calls for a nice cup of tea. What do you say?"

"A cup of Barry's best," answered old Matt.

"Yes," said Gran. "Everyday should have its golden moments."

CHAPTER 25
MY PAL BATES

"You know what, Gran?" I said that night, as I sat on the edge of the bed. "I'm going to ring Bates."

"Bates?" she queried. "I thought you didn't like him."

"It's not a case of like or dislike, I just think he might be able to help us."

"Why so?" she asked.

"Because he's got a special head that holds pucks of information."

She looked at me quizzically. "Okay, but what are you going to ask him?"

"I'm going to ask him about the Torrens System."

"Well," she said as she left the room, "there's no harm in asking."

I dialled his number.

"Hi Bates," I said casually. "How are things?"

"What things?" he asked.

"Oh nothing, just saying hello," I replied.

"Who's this anyway?" he asked.

"This is Emily," I answered. "You sat beside me on the plane and we got lost together down Deborah Central Mine, remember?"

"Oh you," he said. "What do you want?"

I felt like putting down the phone, but I pressed on.

"Can you tell me about the Torrens System in Australia?" I asked, and, immediately, my brilliant pal launched into an explanation.

"The Torrens System is a system through which properties are registered by the state. Land ownership is transferred through registration of title instead of using deeds."

"I don't understand," I said, and I heard Bates muttering to himself at the other end of the phone before answering.

"Common law was the system used before the Torrens system. It meant that when a person bought land, he had to have documents showing the names of the previous owners, and the documents had to prove that the property had been given to the first owner by the government."

"Documents?" I asked.

"In common law, when the first settlers came to Australia, the government granted land to people. This was recorded on a sheet of paper called a document. After that, each time the land was sold, another document was added to the original document. These documents were known as 'title deeds' or 'the chain of title'.

I waited. "And the Torrens System?"

"The common law system caused a lot of legal problems and was replaced by the Torrens System," he replied.

"Which means?" I prompted.

"That today, registrations of properties are kept in a central place in Melbourne, so anybody can access information about a property on the web."

"That helps, thank you,"

"Okay," said Bates, and he hung up.

I turned to Granny, who'd just come into the room again. "That fellow is incredible," I said. "How does he know everything?"

"An amazing person," replied Granny nodding. "And so free with his information."

"He knows all the difficult things, but he just doesn't pick up on the simple things. I just don't get it."

"Well," said Gran, "people like him are very special, and they need to be understood and appreciated in a very special way."

"In the mine," I said, trying to explain, "he said that his head was constructed differently... that it had more space for information, but less space for other things."

"I imagine," commented Granny, "that he didn't explain his inability to empathise with others."

"Empathise?" I asked, screwing up my face.

"People like Bates can be extraordinarily intelligent, but have little or no ability to share happiness, sadness, fun or feelings with other people," she replied.

"Is that why he's so abrupt?" I asked.

Granny smiled. "Probably. It affects people differently."

"So he finds it hard to have a laugh with someone," I said.

"Something like that," Gran responded. "Life can be a lonely place for people like Bates."

I found myself pondering what Granny had told me. Then I got sick of pondering and decided to look up the Torrens System online, as Bowman had suggested, and find out about Rainbow End. And you've guessed correctly. Bates was absolutely spot on with his information.

But, unfortunately, there wasn't any property registered to Mr Patrick O'Neill.

CHAPTER 26
CHURCH

That night, I couldn't sleep.

I turned on one side. I turned on the other side. I lay on my back. I lay on my tummy. I pulled up the duvet. I threw off the duvet. I buried my head in the pillow and counted thousands of sheep, but still I couldn't sleep. I got a drink of water, I said my prayers, I closed my eyes, but still I couldn't sleep.

So I stopped trying to go to sleep and I decided to become fully awake.

I lay in my bed and stretched myself out like a starfish, putting my hands and feet into the four corners of the bed. I stared into the nothingness above me and contemplated.

My nugget of gold was gone, probably stolen. We'd searched everywhere, and it was nowhere to be found. The fact of the matter was that my nugget of gold was history. It was awful, but there was nothing I could do about it. It had vanished, without a trace. I realised it was gone, so there was no use moaning about it anymore. What I couldn't understand was why I was tossing and turning in the bed? I lay as still as I could and let my mind unravel.

Suddenly, I realised that it had something to do with Rainbow End, something to do with Mr Bowman, something to do with the phone call I had overheard, something to do with the note I'd gotten from Mei Ling, and something to do with the value of the property. I knew, without question, that something wasn't quite right, but I just couldn't figure out what exactly was wrong.

I waited again, hoping for inspiration, but nothing came.

I must have dozed off because, next minute, or what seemed like the next minute, I heard Gran's voice, "Rise and shine," and I could feel the words dragging me from my slumber.

"Do I have to?" I groaned.

"It's Sunday," came the sound of Gran's cheerful voice. "Church is at eleven, and that's not early."

"Do I have to go?"

"Absolutely, my dear," she said, as she pulled the duvet off me. "It will be good for your soul."

"Hmm," I muttered, as I curled myself up a bit tighter.

I didn't mind going to church, I just wasn't partial to the rising and shining bit. But Granny was very persistent and, a few moments later, I obliged and got up. We had decided to go to the church where Pa had been 'saved', and I was curious to discover what an Australian service was like.

The church turned out to be a low-lying brick building with a cross on the front. I found the service a bit old-fashioned, but the people were very welcoming. After the service, there was a cup of tea and a chat. Granny struck up a grand conversation with another lady, and I was by myself when I spied an old man in a wheelchair. He was stretching his hand out to reach a creamy bun on the far side of the table but he couldn't quite get it.

"Having a spot of trouble?" I asked cheekily, passing him the plate of buns.

"Ah," he said, twinkling as he caught my eye. "Just creating an opportunity to make a friend." He bit into the bun. "What's your name?"

"I'm Emily McCleary. And yourself?" I asked, politely.

"I'm John Wu. What brings you to this part of the world?"

And, after that, I don't remember exactly what he asked me, except I just found myself talking away to him. He listened to me – really listened to me – and I told him everything.

I told him about Pa working in the mine and being thrown into jail for stealing the nugget of gold. I told him about finding the will behind the cupboard, and the terrible disappointment when Granny discovered that Pa had no Certificate of Title. I told Mr Wu everything. It just came bubbling out and I couldn't stop. The more he nodded and smiled at me, the more I talked. That was the effect he had on me and, when I finished, he looked directly at me.

"My," he said, "that is some story." He continued to eat his bun, savouring the taste of each bite and, every now and again, he'd smile across at me and give me a wink. I knew he was reflecting.

"I don't suppose you have that map with you?" he said at last.

I produced the wrinkled up map and he examined it carefully.

"That's interesting," he said looking at the map. "It's dated 1859. I haven't seen such an old, handwritten map for a long time." He scratched his head as he continued to peer at the map.

"I think your lawyer may have been looking for the land ownership deeds in the wrong place."

"What do you mean?" I asked.

"If you get your Granny, I'll try to explain my thoughts to you both." I collected her and returned promptly, leading her by the hand.

"Granny, this is Mr Wu. He wants to say something to us."

"Your granddaughter has been telling me your story," he said.

"Oh," said Granny. "I hope she hasn't bored you."

"On the contrary! I have been fascinated by the saga, and she has just shown me a very interesting item."

"The map," said Gran, seeing it stretched across his lap.

"Yes," he replied. "It's dated 1859 – rather rare in the new country."

"I suppose," agreed Gran.

He pointed to the name of the law firm in the corner. "See the name Carruthers and Sons LTD, Bendigo? That's where I worked many years ago."

Granny looked at the map.

"It is possible that the ownership titles might be held there."

"Good gracious," said Gran.

"Well they weren't online," I said, interrupting the conversation. Mr Wu looked at me quizzically. "When Granny got ratty with Bowman on the phone, he told her to check the Melbourne register for Pa's Certificate."

"That would have been regular practice," said Mr Wu. "I'm guessing that you checked and they weren't there?"

"No, they weren't. But shouldn't Bowman have checked too?" I asked.

"Of course," replied my new friend.

"Well," I said, thinking hard. "Perhaps you'd ask one of the lawyers if the title deeds are in the office."

Mr Wu turned to Gran and winked. "You've got a very able project manager here, Mrs Clancy. Yes, of course I'd be pleased to look into this situation for you. Since, as a young man, I worked with Carruthers and Sons LTD, I think I could call in a few favours from some colleagues."

"So you're a real lawyer," I said, my face reddening with embarrassment. "I thought you were just working there."

"The wheelchair doesn't affect my brain, you know," he said, with a wry smile.

I was mortified. "Of course not," I said. "I just thought…"

"It's okay," he said. "The wheelchair has its advantages. It makes friends." He smiled and then he looked at Gran. "Would you like me to give you a ring if I unearth any further information?"

"Yes," said Gran, "we would be very grateful. We're in the Shamrock Hotel."

"And here's our Skype," I said, giving him another of my scraps of paper. "Thanks."

CHAPTER 27
QUESTIONS

I was very glad that Mr Wu was checking out Carruthers and Sons LTD, because something was not right. In fact, every fibre in my body told me that something was seriously wrong. I could feel it, but I didn't know what to do next. Then it struck me. It was time to contact my mastermind friend again. He'd be able to explain things clearly for me.

I whipped out my mobile as we left the church. It was down on battery, but I pulled Bates' number up and began to tap at speed:

I turned to Granny. "Something is wrong. Not sure what, but I've asked Bates to help."

"Okay," she replied. "What do you want me to do?"

"Drive to the Golden Dragon Museum. We're meeting Bates at two."

She took one look at me and told me to jump in, and away we sped into the centre of Bendigo.

We arrived at two o'clock on the dot, and there was Bates and his mother deep in conversation with a tall man.

Bates raised a finger as we approached. The man was explaining that Sun Loong, the longest imperial dragon in the world at 100 metres, and his comrade Loong, the longest dragon in the world, both lived in the museum. He was saying that it took fifty-two people plus fifty-two other helpers to carry Sun Loong, and that the dragon was covered in 4,500 scales, 90,000 mirrors, 30,000 beads and his head weighed 29kg.

It was all very fascinating, but I wanted to talk to Bates.

The man continued talking. He explained that, before the dragon first appeared in the 1970 parade, he was blessed and brought to life by an old man who dotted his dragon eyes with chicken blood – a sort of Chinese ritual involving lions and dragons. He was just about to describe Loong when I could bare it no longer and I interrupted. "Excuse me, Bates. Could we talk?"

"Yes," he said, turning around.

"I've a few questions I want answered."

"Have you got any Werther's?"

"No, I haven't."

"And I haven't any answers," he replied, turning back to the man, who proceeded to explain that Loong was built of silk, mirrors, bamboo and papier mâché.

Then I heard Gran's voice. "But she's got a whole bag of liquorice."

Bates turned around again. "So, what are your questions?"

I handed him the map. "You know that Granny was left a property called Rainbow End. This is a map of the place. She doesn't have any deeds. Where would she find them?"

He scanned the map. "In this law firm," he said, pointing to the name of Carruthers and Sons LTD. "The map is dated 1859, so the deeds aren't in Melbourne."

"Are you sure?" I asked.

"Before 1862, when the Torrens System was put in place, title deeds were kept in the local community."

"What do you mean?"

"Rainbow End is probably a General Law Title. Landowners didn't have to change the old titles into the Torrens System, so the titles of some old places stayed in the local lawyer's office files."

"Oh," I said. "Now I understand why Mr Wu is looking for the deeds in Carruthers and Sons."

"Any other questions?" he asked, beginning to walk away.

"They're not questions, but I want your opinion."

"Okay," he replied, politely turning around.

"Well, when I was in with the lawyer, I overheard him telling the estate agent that Gran didn't know the value of the property. Why would he have said that?"

He contemplated. "He probably wants to buy it at a cheap price and sell it on at a better price."

"He told Gran that there weren't any deeds anywhere," I said.

Bates stared ahead. "He's a crook. He has probably already taken over the property and is in the business of re-selling it. Anything else?"

"My friend Mei Ling wrote to me that the mining company wanted to buy it. Would that be possible?"

"Probably," Bates replied, getting bored. "Why don't you ask her?"

"He's right, as usual," I said to Gran, wondering why I hadn't decided to do that in the first place. "Thanks, Bates."

"By the way," said Bates, as he moved over to talk to the tall man again, "you can keep your box of liquorice. I don't like the stuff."

Gran looked at me and we burst out laughing.

"Incorrigible," she whispered.

"But rarely wrong," I whispered back. "Thanks, Bates."

I swung Granny around and walked her quickly to the car. "We've got to talk to Mei Ling... straight away. I'll text her."

The Chan family were at the Joss House Temple. It was a place where the miners used to pray to General Kwan and ask for success in the minefields. As we went in the door, we saw Mei Ling kneeling down with her parents. We joined in, and I said a quick prayer to get my nugget, and for Granny to get Rainbow End. No harm in asking, I thought.

Suddenly, Mei Ling spotted us and came over. "Hello again," she said with a big smile. "I'm glad you text."

"Me too," I replied, "I've something important to ask you."

"Go on..."

"When you wrote in your card, you said that you hoped the mining company would buy Rainbow End. What did you mean?"

"Oh," she replied, blushing. "My dad was really annoyed about that."

"Annoyed about what?" asked her father, coming up behind her.

I looked him straight in the eye. "Mr Chan," I said, "may I ask you something?"

"Certainly," he replied.

"Is the mining company buying Rainbow End?"

He returned my look. "Yes," he replied. "The mining company has made an offer."

"What?" I heard Gran gasp. "We didn't hear anything about this!"

She looked at Mr Chan. "Why didn't you mention it when I was speaking to you?"

"The mining company has been involved in a business deal to purchase Rainbow End for some time now. I didn't mention it, Mrs Clancy, because I was surprised to discover that you thought you were the owner of the property. I was led to believe that the property was jointly owned by a lawyer and a local business man."

I piped up, "Named?"

"Mr Bowman and Mr Kent."

"What?!" Gran exclaimed, leaning against the wall for support.

Mr Chan spoke gravely. "The mining company is currently in the process of buying Rainbow End from them. We've made a good offer."

"And when did you make the offer?" I asked.

"Last month," Mr Chan replied.

"But..." Gran said, at a loss for words, "that was before we came to Australia."

I interrupted again, suddenly remembering something. "Do they have a Certificate of Title?"

"Following my discussion with your grandmother, the matter is under research, but I am assured that everything is in order."

"Well, everything is not in order," I said. "Granny owns Rainbow End. Bowman and Kent are crooks."

"That is correct," said Granny, finding herself able to speak again. "Those men are criminals."

"That's quite an accusation," replied Mr Chan. "Perhaps you should consult your lawyer before..."

Gran interrupted, "My lawyer," she stuttered, "is Mr Bowman."

There was silence. A long silence. Then Mr Chan bowed to Gran. "I'm glad we've had an opportunity to speak," he said. "This situation obviously needs to be investigated." He beckoned to Mei Ling and her mother.

"Come along," he said. "I need to make some phone calls." He bowed to Granny again. "The mining company will definitely be looking carefully into this situation. We'll be in touch."

Gran sat down on a nearby bench and polished her glasses as she thought.

"What will we do now, Granny?" I asked.

"We'll talk to our lawyer," she replied.

"Mr Bowman?" I said, in amazement. "That thief?"

"Of course not," she said. "We'll talk to Mr Wu. Come on, Emily. Will you be able to get him on Skype for me?"

CHAPTER 28
THE FRAUD

We hardly spoke on the way back to the hotel. I climbed the stairs two at a time, switched on the computer and pressed the Skype button for Mr Wu.

"Mr Wu is online," I said, as his face appeared on screen.

My Granny is usually a little anxious about anything to do with the computer, but not this time. She came over to the computer. "Hello Mr Wu," she said. "This is May Clancy."

"Good afternoon to you," he replied, and he didn't get a chance to say anything else until Gran and I had told him all about our conversation with Mr Chan.

"You've certainly had a bit of a shock," he said at the end of her story.

"That would be an understatement," Gran replied. "I can't believe what's happening."

"Well, I've done a little bit of detective work on your behalf, and I've got some news for you."

"Oh," said Gran. "Is it good or bad?"

He paused. "Both. When I got in contact with an old colleague who still works at Carruthers, I discovered that the relevant documents which relate to Rainbow End are actually held in the law firm."

"That's extremely good news," Gran continued, "You're sure about this?"

"Absolutely certain, and Patrick O'Neill's signature is written on the Chain of Deeds."

"That is wonderful news," said Gran, clasping her hands.

"So that proves that Pa did own Rainbow End?" I asked.

"That is correct," replied Mr Wu. "And my inquiries also led me to discover that Bowman is a member of the Carruthers law firm, and that Bowman and a real estate agent were making inquiries about jointly registering this property under the Torrens System."

"Just give me a moment," Gran said, her head going into top gear. "Are you telling me what I think you're telling me?"

"I think so," said Mr Wu. "It seems that the property, Rainbow End has recently become very important for the Gold Mining Company, strategically, as it gives easy access to a gold-bearing reef in the area." He paused.

I glanced at Gran.

"So that's why Mr Chan was interested in it," she murmured.

"Yes," Mr Wu replied. "As a result of an interest expressed by the Gold Mining Company in the past year, a search was conducted by Bowman to establish ownership of the property."

"Of course," murmured Granny.

"To Bowman's utter delight," Mr Wu continued, "he discovered that the property of Rainbow End wasn't registered with the Victoria Land Register, nobody had lived on the property for fifty years, the owner had disappeared without trace, and the chain of deeds connected with the property was held in the very law firm where he worked. He obviously couldn't believe his luck."

I was in like a shot, "So he thought nobody owned the place, and he could steal it?"

"Yes," replied Mr Wu. "Bowman saw an opportunity to acquire the land and sell it on to the Gold Mining Company at an exorbitant price."

"Wow!" I said. So, Bates was right again.

"It's unbelievable," Gran muttered.

"But how did Kent get in on the act?" I asked, butting in yet again.

"I'm just guessing," replied Mr Wu, "but maybe he discovered Bowman's involvement in the situation and threatened to expose him if he didn't get a half share."

"What crooks!" I said, thinking how fast Bates had been able to understand the situation.

"And they never thought we'd turn up," Gran muttered.

"There's still something I don't understand," I said. "At first, Bowman was going to sell Rainbow End for us."

"For a sum that I'd think was fantastic," said Gran.

"But then he changed his mind and pretended that Granny wasn't the rightful owner so he couldn't sell the land for her at all. Why did he change his plan?" I asked.

"Carruthers and Sons is a reputable firm," Mr Wu explained, "and Bowman obviously became concerned that, if it was known that your Gran was the vendor, the sale of a valuable property for a small sum of money would attract attention. So he wanted you to go home to Ireland as soon as possible so they could quietly register the property."

Mr Wu paused. "But they have a problem... A huge problem. They are under enormous pressure to register the property, because an auction is being held next Friday to sell the place. This was organised before you came to Australia because the mining company were pressing to purchase the place."

Gran reached for a glass of water.

"It seems that the transfer of the property hasn't gone through yet, and Bowman and Kent may have to use bogus papers for the auction," continued Mr Wu.

"So what can we do?" asked Gran.

"We'll have to expose Kent and Bowman," Mr Wu said soberly.

"But how?" Gran asked.

Suddenly, I had a bright idea. "I know," I said turning to Mr Wu. "Can't you pretend that you want to buy the property? You could pretend that you're from a mining company in South Africa who wants to buy Rainbow End."

"But how would that help matters?" he asked.

"Well, if you wanted to buy it, they'd have to show you the papers and you could have them checked out properly."

"Better again," said Gran, "you could ask to check out the papers at the auction so these swindlers would be publically exposed."

Mr Wu paused again and smiled. Then he looked directly at me.

"A plan worth considering. You have a clever granny," he said. "I'll get into action straight away. Goodbye for now." And he switched off Skype.

CHAPTER 29
THE AUCTION

I could feel the butterflies in my tummy. The day of the auction had arrived. It was being held in a private room in the Shamrock. The plan was that Granny and I were to stay out of the auction room until the auction began, because we didn't want Mr Bowman and Mr Kent to suspect anything strange was going on.

Up in our room, Granny drank loads of coffee and I drank loads of orange as we waited for Mr Bowman and Mr Kent to arrive. Every now and again, I squinted out the window. There seemed to be quite a lot of people coming to the auction. At quarter to one, three men approached the hotel. I recognised two of them. Mr Bowman was walking slightly behind Mr Kent, and behind them was a small, squat bald man.

I rang Mr Wu. "They're on their way."

"Just Mr Bowman and Mr Kent?"

"There's another man too."

"Good. That's the auctioneer. Thanks for the call. Wait for a few minutes before you come down."

I slipped the phone back in my pocket. "We're to go down, Gran, in a few minutes. Are you ready?"

"All ready to go," she said, tapping her handbag.

Downstairs, the auction was just about to begin. We slipped in the back and sat down beside the window. The auctioneer was sitting behind a table at the front, and I could see Mr Bowman and Mr Kent sitting in the second row. Eventually, the auctioneer stood up.

"Well, as you all know, we're here for the sale of Rainbow End. This property has sparked considerable interest," the auctioneer said, "and I am sure that everybody in this room is fully aware that the property provides access to the newly discovered gold-bearing reef." He paused. "In fact," he continued, "it is the most valuable piece of property to come on the market for many years. Now, I presume you've all read the conditions of sale." He looked around. "Rainbow End will be sold to the highest bidder, and the purchaser will be required to pay a deposit on the fall of the hammer. The sale and contracts will be completed within twenty-eight days."

I glanced up at Granny. She was sitting very upright in the chair, and her lips were in a straight line.

The auctioneer bunched his eyebrows together. "But, before we commence the sale, does anybody have any questions regarding the title or the maps or any other documentation material to the sale of this property?"

There was silence. Then Mr Wu spoke up. "Before the bidding commences, I wonder would you clarify for me the name of the current owners of Rainbow End."

"No problem at all," replied the auctioneer. "Rainbow End is the property of Mr Bowman and Mr Kent."

"And the certificate of title is in order?" Mr Chan asked.

"Right here on the table in front of me."

"Well," Mr Wu said, "there is a lady here who wishes to contest the title."

The auctioneer looked very uncomfortable. "I'm afraid this is a bit out of order."

"I don't care whether it's out of order or not," said Gran, standing up tall. "I have something to say and I'm going to say it."

Everybody turned around as Granny walked slowly up to the front of the room. She was clutching her red leather bag tightly under her arm. She stopped directly in front of the auctioneer. "Excuse me," she said loudly and clearly. "I have here in my bag proof that I am the vendor."

There was silence in the room.

"This man," she said, pointing to Mr Bowman, "and his friend, Mr Kent, are impostors."

"That's a very serious allegation," said the auctioneer.

"You're absolutely right about that, and I'm going to tell you exactly why."

There was a shuffle as all the people sat up in their seats.

"Madam," said the auctioneer, taking a step towards her. "I can see that we'll have to postpone this auction until these matters are clarified."

"No," said Gran. "We'll clarify them right now."

There was a general murmur from everybody as the auctioneer tried politely to get Granny to sit down. Then Mr Chan spoke up.

"Let's hear this woman speak. She has travelled from Ireland to establish her right to the property. Let's hear what she has to say." Then he bowed to Granny. She gave him a little thank you nod, and waited for silence.

"My father, Patrick Hannigan," she said, "came to Australia with my mother and, in 1945, they purchased Rainbow End."

People settled into their seats to listen.

"My father was thrown into prison for theft... for stealing gold from the mine."

Everybody was listening keenly.

"For two years, he was incarcerated for a crime he didn't commit. During that time, my mother, who was sick, returned to Ireland with me." Gran paused, and the people waited. "She never saw her husband again."

Somebody's pen fell on the floor.

"She died, and I was raised by aunts." Gran took a deep breath.

"My father thought I had died, too, and it was many years before I met him again. He was an old man in a nursing home then, and I didn't even recognise him."

The pen rolled down along the wooden floor.

"Even after all those years, he knew me." Gran stopped. "He knew me, but he never told me who he was. Thought I'd be ashamed of him."

The pen stopped at her feet. She bent down and picked it up.

There was absolute silence in the room.

"And, in his will, he left me Rainbow End... and I have the proof."

You could hear a pin drop.

Gran opened her bag, took out the will and the chain of deeds, and placed them on the table.

"There's the proof."

All of a sudden, the noise level began to rise. People shifted in their seats as they turned to talk to the people beside them. The auctioneer was shuffling the papers on the table. Mr Bowman was looking furtively around and Mr Chan was stretching out his hand to pick up the will when, all of a sudden, I noticed that Mr Kent was missing.

I looked around. There wasn't a sign of him. He had been in the room when Granny and I came in, but where was he now? Where had he disappeared to?

I quickly left and made my way to the main entrance and, as I reached the door, I spotted Mr Kent skirting around the corner of the building at great speed.

I started to follow him. I began to run. Down the street I ran, down past the shops, down past the houses, falling over dogs, bumping against people as I wove my way in and out. The gap between us was widening. What was I to do? I ran faster until I thought my lungs would burst, but the gap continued to widen. I could see that Mr Kent was heading for his green Ute, which was parked near the railway line.

I'm not slow, but I knew I hadn't a chance of catching up with him. Time to use my brain, so I stopped and did what all children do to get attention. I took a deep breath, opened my mouth, and hollered at the top of my voice. "Stop that thief! Stop that thief!"

People stopped in the street. I kept screaming. They looked at me in amazement, they looked at the escaping Mr Kent in amazement, and then they looked back at me, but nobody moved to stop the thief.

Then, in the distance, out of the corner of my eye, I saw Bates. He was down the street, peering through a shop window reading something.

"Bates," I screamed.

Bates looked up.

"Stop that man."

And, without batting an eyelid, he stuck out his leg. His timing was perfect. In full flight, Mr Kent simply could not stop. He tripped right over Bates' extended leg and fell flat on his nose, and there he lay, sprawled out on the pavement.

With a great effort, I ran to the spot where he lay, half dazed. "Going somewhere?" I panted.

Mr Kent levered himself up. A curious crowd had begun to gather. He looked past me at the watchful faces.

"Somewhere far away?" I inquired.

The crowd began to gather in closer.

"In a hurry?" I asked, playing for time.

Mr Kent's eyes narrowed as he stood up, dusted himself down and scanned around for an escape route. "To the station," he said to the crowd. "Excuse me."

And, moving towards a young woman, he explained, "I've a train to catch."

He stepped forward and the crowd parted.

I began to panic. "He's a thief. Don't let him go."

"I won't," the woman replied, and I suddenly noticed that she was wearing a light blue police shirt. "We've been waiting to interview this gentleman for quite some time."

"And he's certainly going to the station," her colleague beside her added, producing some handcuffs, "but I'm afraid it's not a train station." He turned to Mr Kent,

"You've a few questions to answer. You and your friend Mr Bowman."

Then Mr Kent, covered in dust, was led away and, as he passed, we locked eyes.

"Not bad," he spat. "Not bad for a baby!" And then that horrible man was gone.

I looked at Bates. "Nice move."

He nodded, and then he turned back to continue reading whatever he had been reading. I stared at him.

"If it wasn't for you, we'd never have caught them." I said.

He gave a little shrug.

"You're an ace," I added.

"Hmm," he muttered, sticking his nose up against the pane.

"We did it, you know."

"Did what?" he said, giving me a quick glance. "You haven't got the gold, have you?" And, with that, he bent down to peer intently at some minute writing on some shabby old book in the window, and I was forgotten.

"We got the thieves," I growled, trying to grab the last bit of his attention, but already he had retreated into his own world and was filling his head with information. He hadn't seemed to notice the gathering crowd, or the excitement. The arrest of Mr Kent and Mr Bowman hadn't seemed to interest him.

I stood glued to the ground. The crowd was beginning to move away and suddenly I felt blank, and my legs began to shake. In fact, everything began to go wobbly. And then I saw Gran walking towards me. She had her arms open wide to give me a hug. I ran towards her, and she put her arms around me.

"You were absolutely fantastic," she whispered in my ear.

And then, all of a sudden, I felt fantastic, absolutely fantastic. Bates and I had saved the day, even if Bates hadn't noticed. The two crooks were under arrest and everything could be sorted out.

I closed my eyes and snuggled into Gran and, when I opened them again, I spotted Mr Wu smiling at me. "And you'll restore the property to its rightful owners?" I said.

"Without a doubt," he replied. "It would give me great pleasure."

"And you'll be able to sell Rainbow End to the real gold mining company for us too?"

"If that's your grandmother's wish," he replied.

And as Gran released me, she gave a little chortle. "I think you can safely say that I would be delighted to engage Mr Wu's services for the task ahead." Then she smiled at Mr Wu. "You've no idea," she said, "how glad I am that my granddaughter made your acquaintance on Sunday."

"Me too," I added, wondering if we'd see a lot more of Mr Wu in the future.

CHAPTER 29
HOME SWEET HOME

Our holiday was nearly over. It was time to say goodbye. I knew Gran felt sad as Rainbow End disappeared into the distance for the last time, but Rainbow End had been sold, and now we were going home. Granny would be able to pay off all the debts and she wouldn't have to worry about the bills anymore.

I looked across at her as we sped down the Calder Freeway back to Melbourne airport. She'd said she would share her crock of gold with me. How I loved my Gran. Reading my thoughts, she said, "And I love you, too, Emily, and love is the real wealth in life."

Just then, I noticed a huge wedge-tailed eaglehawk by the side of the road and, as we passed, he rose into the air. I'd never seen such a bird. He stretched his wings and they seemed to fill the road. He looked powerful as he drew his large body up, and folded his talons underneath. His curved beak tilted slightly as he watched me with his yellow eyes before he disappeared into the blue sky. I kept watching him until he became a tiny spec in the distance.

"Another golden moment to treasure," Granny murmured and I knew what she meant.

The journey seemed to go very quickly. I just slept, ate, read books and watched films, and, twenty-four hours later, we arrived at our cottage. The daffodils in the window boxes were just about to bloom, and the birds were eating the last of the coconut.

"Oh it's good to be home," said Gran, as she unlocked the door. The place smelled musty and everything felt damp, but it was home and I was looking forward to seeing all my friends again.

"We'll just light the fire and it'll be all snug in half an hour," said Gran with a big smile.

We wheeled in our suitcases and I had just stuck my case behind the door when Granny tripped over the mat. I thought she'd hurt herself, but she just picked herself up and told me to give her a hand pushing the mat under the cupboard. "So no one else trips over it," she said.

I walked over to the cupboard. It was still sticking out since the time I'd poked out the will from behind it. We tried to stick the mat under it but it was stuck.

"Perhaps, if you bent down and pushed, we'd be able to move it," Gran suggested.

I did as I was told and, as I bent, I spotted something jammed behind the press.

"Oops!" I said, getting the brush and poking at the object.

"There's the culprit," I said, pulling out something that looked like a stone and handing it to Gran. She took it and turned it over in her palm. Then, all of a sudden, she became very quiet.

"Good gracious," she said as she walked to the sink, turned on the tap and put the thing under the water. Then she got some soap and began to scrub.

"Good gracious," she said for the second time. "I don't believe it."

"Don't believe what?" I asked.

"I recognise this."

"What do you mean?" I asked, peering at the soapy object.

"Look, look," she said, putting it under the tap. "Can you see the way it's beginning to sparkle?"

I looked, and suddenly I realised what she meant. My heart started pounding.

"Granny," I whispered. "Is it the nugget of gold? Pa's nugget of gold?"

"My word," she said to herself, and I could see her heart was pounding too. "It's not possible."

She lifted the nugget up to the light and tilted it in all directions. "I can't believe it... but it's just as I remember it... It's the one I used to play with all those years ago.

I thought my heart would burst.

"He had it all the time," she said in disbelief. She gazed at it. "The elusive nugget of gold. We have it at last," she said, as her eyes began to fill up. Then she passed it to me. I looked at it in my hand. It was lumpy and smooth and heavy.

"It must have fallen behind the sideboard when he was falling." I whispered.

I turned it over in my hand. I could feel everything inside me shaking with excitement as I examined the gold. It wasn't an enormous nugget. In fact, it was a small nugget and it didn't look very shiny, but it was mine. My present from Pa.

I thought of all the fabulous times we'd had in Australia. I thought about all the people we'd met on our travels – Mei Ling and her parents, Kira the Aborigine, Matt the fiddler, Mr Bowman and Mr Kent, the two crooks, and of course Mr Wu, the wheelchair lawyer. And then I thought of Bates and the time we got lost down the mine and, all of a sudden, I could see the outline of the Lady Deborah in my mind. I could see her old-fashioned clothes and the bun on top of her head. She was smiling at me as she held up her lamp, and I could hear the old miner's words ringing in my ears.

"Mark my words," he was saying, "there'll be gold found in the near future."

I put my hand in my pocket, pulled out my phone, scrolled down to B, and pressed.

I heard the ring tone as he picked up.

"Bates," I said, my voice cracking with excitement. "The prophecy has come true."

There was silence.

"I found the gold. It was behind the cupboard."

There was a pause, and then he asked, "And has it been verified?"

All of a sudden, finding the pyrite with Kira flashed into my mind.

"All that glitters is not gold!" he said.

My heart sank. The metal detector had found the pyrite at Rainbow End.

"Was it authenticated? Checked out?" he inquired.

"How should I know?" I stammered.

"Well," he said, and I knew he was about to switch off, "let me know, when you know."

The maggot was right, as usual. I opened my fist slowly. The nugget was gleaming and glistening in the centre of my palm. It looked like gold, it felt like gold, but was it gold? Real gold?

I touched it gingerly.

"Bite it," my gran said. "Put it in your mouth and bite it, hard."

Puzzled, I did as I was told and crunched my nugget.

"Now, take a look," she said.

I looked, and I saw the ugly imprint of my teeth.

"It's an old miner's trick." Granny smiled. "Real gold is soft."

I put my hand in my pocket and pulled out my phone. I scrolled down to B again, and pressed.

Bates picked up.

"It's gold," I said. "Real Bendigo Gold."

Dear Readers,

If you're in a circle of readers or if somebody is reading this book to you, here are a few things to chat about:

1. What type of person is Emily? How does her character change as the story progresses?
2. How would you describe the relationship between Granny and Emily?
3. How would you describe the relationships between Emily and the other adults in the book?
4. What do you think of Bates? Do you know people like Bates? Having read the book, would you have a different attitude to people like him? Why?
5. Mei Ling doesn't appear very often in the book, but why is she so important in regard to Granny's inheritance?
6. The Aborigines lived in Australia for many years before the Europeans arrived. What do you learn about their culture from Alkira?
7. The ghost story about Lady Deborah tells how the ghost is the harbinger of good news. Why has this story

been put inside the bigger story? Are ghosts real? Are they scary? Do they help people?

8. What were the differences between Tess Bryan and Emily McCleary? What were the similarities?

9. Can you find the following in the book? Dialogue, a will, an announcement, a diary, text messages, a Skype chat, a story, a letter, a quiz and a telephone conversation. What makes each of these different?

Find out more at
www.bendigogold.weebly.com

Informative

Bendigo Gold is full of information about Australia. What did you discover about: wildlife; gold mining; the early pioneers; land ownership; the tourist trail in Bendigo; people with special needs; superstitions; the Aborigines; people in the 1940s; and people today.

Persuasive

What language did the author use to persuade you that Mr Bowman was an unpleasant person?

How did Mr Kent persuade Granny to trust him?

What strategy did Emily use to persuade Bates to stop walking when they were lost in the mine?

How did the auctioneer try to persuade people to buy Rainbow End?

Imaginative

Which part of the book do you find most imaginative. Why?

How do the folk stories from other countries arouse your imagination?

Have you ever been in bed trying to go to sleep? Did you feel like Emily?

If you were drawing a picture of the people in the airport in Melbourne, what would you draw?